SWEET REVENGE

A PINK CUPCAKE MYSTERY BOOK 11

HARPER LIN

This is a work of fiction. Names, characters, organizations, places, events, and incidents are either products of the author's imagination or are used fictitiously.

SWEET REVENGE

ISBN: 978-1-987859-99-7

www.harperlin.com

CHAPTER ONE

AMELIA WALISHOVSKY, though she still sometimes caught herself saying "Harley," paused at the curb and took a long, deep breath. The buttery scent of vanilla and sugar drifted through the crisp Oregon morning air, warm and familiar, like a welcome-home hug. Even from a distance, she could tell that The Pink Cupcake was already awake and working its magic.

After two blissful weeks in the Bahamas with Dan, of hammocks, umbrella drinks, and pretending real life didn't exist, she was supposed to feel rested. And she did, mostly.

There had been no orders to fill. No last-minute ingredient substitutions. No one asking for a gluten-free, dairy-free, sugar-free cupcake and then complaining that it didn't taste like a regular one. Her only decisions had been whether to try the mango or passionfruit daiquiri and how much SPF to slather on before a walk along the beach.

It had been paradise. But this was home.

As she looked at the familiar stretch of Food Truck Alley, now bustling with early morning prep, she felt a comforting tug in her chest. Trucks were rolling open their awnings, the usual aroma of barbecue, garlic, and strong coffee mingling in the air. Vendors she knew were setting up with their typical pre-service choreography: stretching cords, firing up grills, wiping down counters, and already exchanging cheerful insults with neighboring food trucks.

Her gaze found The Pink Cupcake immediately. Her own truck. Her pride and joy. It looked like a pastel-colored dream among a lineup of rugged, metallic griddles and deep fryers. The cheery pink paint still held up well against the elements, and the looping white script across the side looked more whimsical than cutesy now. A couple of years ago, she'd worried it was too precious. Now, it was iconic.

She made her way across the lot, her boots crunching softly on the gravel, and spotted movement inside the truck. There was Lila, hunched over her laptop at the narrow side table, her messy ponytail bobbing as she tapped with laser focus. She was probably already knee-deep in inventory spreadsheets or calculating margins to the third decimal.

And there was Beatrice. Covered in flour as usual, standing at the prep counter with the concentration of a sculptor chiseling out a statue from cake batter. Her brow furrowed, her entire body committed to the sacred act of mixing. Only Beatrice could make stirring look heroic.

Amelia smiled. Some things never changed, and thank goodness for that.

She stepped up to the truck and knocked twice on the metal siding, the way she always did, before climbing inside.

Lila didn't even glance up. "Oh good, you're back," she said dryly. "You're officially on duty again."

Amelia snorted. "Nice to see you too, Lila. I missed the warmth."

Beatrice turned from her bowl like she was emerging from a trance, her face grave. She pointed her whisk at Amelia as if delivering a dire warning.

"Do you have *any* idea how many people ask for wedding-themed cupcakes when their cousin's coworker's sister gets engaged?"

Amelia blinked. "Uh... A lot?"

Beatrice threw up her hands, exasperated. "A *ridiculous* amount! I have been asked to make cupcakes that 'represent the couple's journey through life together.' What does that even mean? Am I supposed to bake their childhood memories into buttercream?"

Lila smirked without looking up, her fingers still tapping away at her laptop like a piano virtuoso on deadline. "I told her she should just make two cupcakes and put a fondant bridge between them. 'Journey through life together,' done. Boom. Metaphor accomplished."

Beatrice, never one to let sarcasm pass unchecked, pointed a flour-dusted wooden spoon at her like a teacher delivering a pop quiz. "You laugh, but *I* have been dealing with these people for two weeks. Two. Weeks. Of Pinterest boards and 'vision cupcakes.' Do you know what a 'cupcake mood board' is? Because I do. I've seen one. I've survived one."

Amelia grinned, unwrapping her scarf and hanging it by the back door hook. "So, what I'm hearing is that the truck didn't burn down while I was gone."

Lila snorted. "Barely. You owe me hazard pay. Or at the very least a spa gift card. I've earned a facial just from listening to someone debate whether a rose petal swirl 'truly captures eternal love.'"

Beatrice let out a long, theatrical sigh, setting her spoon down as though the weight of cupcake-related nonsense had finally broken her spirit. "And yet," she said with melodramatic flair, "the real tragedy is that no one was murdered."

Amelia groaned, laughing as she made her way to the sink. "Oh, come on. Can't I go on one vacation without you two acting like I'm the town's designated death magnet?"

Lila and Beatrice exchanged a perfectly timed glance. "No," they said in unison before breaking into laughter.

Amelia rolled her eyes but couldn't help grinning. She washed her hands in the warm water, the scent of vanilla soap and the gentle hiss of the faucet grounding her, tugging her back into routine. She reached for a dish towel, dried her hands, and turned slowly in a little circle, taking in the truck like it was an old friend she hadn't seen in a while.

Everything was exactly how she'd left it. The counter space was lined with her measuring cups and piping bags, all tucked into their proper places. The glass display case gleamed beneath the lights, already stocked with the morning's first batch of cupcakes:

classic vanilla, chocolate ganache, and something pink and sparkly Beatrice had definitely invented in a moment of manic genius. Her recipe notebook sat tucked in its usual corner, its pages just slightly curled from flour-dusted fingertips and years of use.

It was cozy. It was cluttered. It was perfect. She hadn't realized just how much she'd missed this place.

Lila looked up again, her smirk softened into something warmer. "Seriously, though. It's good to have you back."

Beatrice nodded, brushing flour off her apron with a quick swipe. "Agreed. You're the only one who can handle the really difficult customers."

Amelia raised a brow, already sensing the trap. "And by difficult, you mean...?"

Beatrice's face twisted into a grimace. "Oh, you'll see soon enough."

Lila took a sip of her coffee, her eyes glittering with mischief. "Consider it a welcome-back gift."

"Why do I get the feeling my peaceful honeymoon bubble is about to be violently popped?"

Lila raised her cup slightly in a mock toast. "Because it is." She leaned one elbow on the counter, voice casual but loaded. "The whole food truck crew's been talking about your new favorite customer."

Amelia froze mid-wipe of the counter. "That... doesn't sound good."

Beatrice, now transferring a fresh tray of cupcakes into the display case, snorted. "Oh, you're going to *love* this."

Before Amelia could dig for details, a familiar figure appeared outside the window. Kev from The Fry Shack strolled up with his usual confident gait, though today, his easygoing grin was noticeably dimmed by exhaustion.

"Finally back, huh?" he said, shaking his head as he approached. "Good, because I can't deal with Evelyn anymore."

Mina from Curry Express leaned out of her service window across the lot, her long braid swinging like a punctuation mark as she groaned, "Ugh, Evelyn. That woman is a menace."

From the other direction, Big Brad from Smoky B's BBQ looked up from his grill, tongs in one hand, and wiped the other on his smoke-stained apron. His deep voice rumbled across the alley. "She came by last week and said my brisket was—get this—'too smoky.'"

Amelia blinked, genuinely confused. "It's… barbecue."

Brad lifted both hands in disbelief, tongs still flapping. "That's what I said! It's literally *in the name!*"

He looked to the sky like he was hoping for divine intervention, then shook his head and went back to flipping ribs.

"I bet she's still banned from the farmers' market," Kev mumbled.

Mina gave a knowing nod and crossed her arms. "Oh, she is. She got into it with the jam vendor again. Claimed she could taste preservatives in the home-made raspberry preserves."

Amelia raised an eyebrow. "Did she prove it?"

Mina smirked. "Of course not. But that didn't stop her from standing on a crate and shouting, 'Boycott the frauds!' like she was leading a revolution."

Brad gave a gruff laugh and tossed another slab of meat on the grill. "She threatened to call the state agricultural board. Over a jar of jam. A *jam emergency.*"

Kev gave an exaggerated sigh. "I knew she was bad news, but last week? That was peak Evelyn."

Amelia frowned slightly, arms crossed. "Should I even ask what happened?"

Beatrice, sensing the cue like a seasoned stage performer, clapped her hands together, sending a puff of flour into the air as she struck a storytelling pose. "Oh, you missed a good one."

Amelia's shoulders lifted slightly with a preemptive wince. "How bad are we talking?"

Beatrice shook her head. "She threw a fit over a cupcake."

Amelia didn't even try to hide the groan. "Of course she did."

Lila chimed in with a sly smile. "But not just *any* cupcake." She gave Amelia a nudge. "Your honey lavender lemon one."

Amelia's eyes widened. "Wait, that was a new flavor we were testing."

"Yep," Beatrice said, nodding solemnly. "And she called it—" she used air quotes "'an assault on her taste buds.'"

Amelia stared. "You're joking."

Beatrice gestured to herself, covered in flour. "Do I *look* like I'm joking? I spent ten minutes watching that woman poke at it with a fork like it had personally offended her family. She dissected that poor cupcake like she was prepping it for an autopsy."

Kev shook his head. "More like an assault on *our* patience."

Mina let out a soft snort, brushing a crumb from her apron. "Honestly, if she hates everything so much, why does she keep coming back?"

Amelia glanced at Lila, who was already raising an eyebrow.

"Oh, don't worry," Lila said, sipping her coffee. "Something tells me she's *very* invested."

Amelia shook her head, half-laughing despite herself. "Well... I guess I should be flattered she's this obsessed with our recipes."

She tried to laugh it off, to let it land as just another story in a long line of Food Truck Alley dramas.

But deep down, something didn't sit right.

Difficult customers were part of the job. There were always a few who complained too much, or expected their cupcake to fix their emotional baggage. But Evelyn didn't sound like the usual brand of picky or petty. She sounded deliberate. She sounded like trouble.

CHAPTER TWO

THE LUNCH RUSH was in full swing, and The Pink Cupcake thrummed like a well-oiled machine, a pink-and-frosted engine fueled by joy and efficiency.

Outside, the line stretched into a pleasant curve, filled with chattering customers debating their flavor choices, snapping selfies, and posting mid-bite cupcake reviews in real time. The sweet scent of vanilla, sugar, and buttercream swirled in the air.

Inside the truck, Amelia moved with the quiet grace of someone who knew exactly when to step forward and when to get out of the way. She wiped her hands on a towel, the soft feel of the fabric grounding her. The day had unfolded with an almost eerie smoothness: orders rolling in, cupcakes rolling out, no fires, literal or otherwise, to put out.

Beatrice stood at the prep counter like an artist at her canvas, piping buttercream swirls with a focus that bordered on spiritual. Each swirl landed with her signature flourish. Her movements were slow and so precise that Amelia half-expected her to sign her name in icing.

At the front, Lila worked the register like she was conducting a symphony. Tap, swipe, click, smile. She answered customer questions with just the right amount of charm and speed, calculated down to the second.

For one blissful moment, Amelia felt it, that rare, elusive calm that came when every gear clicked into place. She allowed herself to exhale.

And then, like thunder cracking through a blue sky, a voice shattered the peace.

"This is absolutely unacceptable!"

The air inside the truck shifted on a dime.

Beatrice froze mid-squeeze, her piping bag erupting into a fat, squiggly blob that slumped sideways on the cupcake like a deflated hat. Lila's fingers hovered over the touchscreen, frozen mid-transaction. A customer's phone, which had just been capturing a video of their glitter-frosted cupcake, slowly lowered. Even outside the truck, the usual hum of conversation went still. Heads turned. Necks craned. People leaned sideways, rubbernecking toward the service window.

Amelia closed her eyes for half a second and groaned internally. She didn't need to look. She *knew*.

Still, ever the professional, she turned with a practiced smile stretched across her face, warm enough to be polite, cool enough to brace for impact.

It was Evelyn Waters.

There she stood, one perfectly manicured hand clutched a half-eaten cupcake like it was a murder weapon; the other perched indignantly on her hip. Her lipstick, a deep crimson that had somehow gotten smudged at both corners, looked like war paint. Her eyes, narrowed into dagger slits, locked onto Amelia with laser precision.

Amelia felt a familiar prickle of tension rise along her spine. A perfect storm of entitlement, theatrics, and indignation had arrived. She took a calming breath through her nose.

And so it begins.

"Hi there," Amelia said smoothly, her voice dipped in honey. "What seems to be the problem?"

Evelyn held up the sad remains of her cupcake with a dramatic flourish, angling it toward the crowd like she was starring in *Law & Order: Baked Goods Unit*.

"The problem," she declared, her voice pitched to carry, "is that your so-called honey lavender lemon cupcake made me *violently* ill last night." Evelyn's eyes widened with performative suffering. "I was up all night with stomach cramps, and this morning, well, I'll spare you the details, but let's just say it wasn't pretty."

Amelia had heard every cupcake-related complaint imaginable. Too dry, too moist, not enough frosting, too much frosting, not pink enough, too pink. But a food poisoning claim? That was new. And serious.

A quiet hush fell over the line behind Evelyn. The moment was a powder keg. Amelia knew one wrong move could make it explode.

Beatrice, still gripping her piping bag, stiffened. Her hands remained frozen in mid-air, the swirl she'd been piping halfway between masterpiece and disaster. Her voice cut through the tension, low and clipped. "That's strange. We use fresh ingredients, and none of our other customers have complained."

Her tone wasn't defensive; it was factual, cool, and steady. The Beatrice equivalent of raising an eyebrow.

Evelyn scoffed with dramatic flair, tossing her hair back like she was preparing for her close-up. "Well, *I'm* complaining!"

Her voice rose just enough to bounce off the neighboring trucks, sharp and nasal. Amelia saw it happening in real time, the ripple of attention, customers turning their heads, subtle frowns forming as people exchanged puzzled glances.

Amelia sighed inwardly. *That's what she wants,* she thought. *An audience.*

"And I want a full refund," Evelyn continued, projecting like she was auditioning for dinner theater. Her chin lifted, her posture rigid with self-righteousness. "For this and every cupcake I bought last week. I won't be silenced!"

Lila, still a portrait of cool efficiency, let out a breath that was almost inaudible, but Amelia recognized it. It was the sound of a woman mentally canceling her afternoon yoga plans.

"Evelyn," Lila said carefully, in her most measured, customer-service voice, "if you got sick, are you sure it was from our cupcake? It could've been something else you ate."

Evelyn's eyes flashed. "Are you accusing me of *lying?*"

The indignation in her voice was so sharp it practically vibrated.

Amelia stepped in before Lila could say more. She kept her tone professional, her face composed, but inside, she was counting to ten. Twice.

"Of course not," she said evenly. "We take customer concerns very seriously. But if there were an issue with our cupcakes, we'd likely be hearing from other customers, too. We've sold quite a few in the last few days, and no one else has reported anything."

Evelyn didn't budge. Her lips flattened into a razor-thin line. Her eyes narrowed. "So, you're refusing to take responsibility?"

Amelia glanced at Lila, who was now jabbing the register screen a little too pointedly.

"I'm saying," Amelia replied, "that I'd like to understand exactly what happened before jumping to conclusions."

Evelyn leaned in then, inching closer to the service window. Her voice dropped to a whisper, sharp enough to slice fondant.

"Let me spell it out for you," she hissed. "Either you give me my money back, or I will personally make sure no one ever buys from this food truck again." She tilted her head, eyes glinting, her smile smug. "Do you know how many people read my reviews?"

There it was. The actual threat. The heart of the performance. This wasn't about a sour stomach or a refund. This was about control. Evelyn was something else. She wasn't just hoping for a freebie. She was testing them. Testing *Amelia*. How far would she bend?

Amelia straightened her shoulders and drew in a slow breath through her nose, then exhaled just as slowly. Her eyes met Evelyn's and didn't flinch.

"Evelyn," she said, voice firm but not cold, "I can't offer you a refund for an entire week's worth of cupcakes because you *think* one of them made you sick. If you have a doctor's report that proves otherwise, I'd be happy to look into it." A pause. She let the next words land like a gavel. "Until then, I stand by the quality of our product."

Evelyn's expression twisted into something uglier. Her pupils flared, her nostrils flared, and for one wild moment, Amelia wondered if she was about to throw the cupcake remains straight through the window.

"Oh, you'll regret this," Evelyn snapped, her voice low and venomous.

Evelyn stuffed the mangled remains of the

cupcake into a Ziplock bag, and then into her over-sized designer handbag with all the flair of someone preserving crucial evidence for a courtroom showdown.

"I will be speaking to my lawyer," she declared. Then with a sharp theatrical pivot, she spun on her heel and stormed off, the clack of her stilettos on the pavement echoing. As she stalked away, she muttered loud enough to be heard, tossing out phrases like "disgraceful service" and "gross negligence" with the casual venom.

Behind her, the line of customers shifted, leaned close to each other with hushed tones and raised eyebrows. Some looked concerned. Others intrigued. A few clearly just wanted their cupcakes and not the drama. But regardless of the reaction, Evelyn had gotten exactly what she came for. Attention.

Amelia's stomach twisted in the aftermath. She inhaled slowly, willing the tension to slide off her shoulders. The moment Evelyn disappeared around the corner of the lot, swallowed by the crowd and the distant hum of traffic, the spell broke.

Beatrice let out a sharp breath, like someone who had been holding her own commentary in with both fists.

"Well," she muttered, setting down her piping bag, "that was fun."

"Like a root canal," Lila added, still staring at the register as if hoping the touchscreen might dissolve and take the memory of Evelyn with it. "Not a single other person has complained about the honey lavender lemon cupcakes. She's the only one."

A few customers edged closer to the window, hesitant but still hungry.

Lila cleared her throat and turned back to the register. "Next in line?"

Beatrice picked up her piping bag again like nothing had happened, though her shoulders were still a little stiff. "Who's up for a double chocolate swirl?"

The rhythm resumed, but the tension still buzzed in the air.

When the line died down, Kev from The Fry Shack leaning casually against his own truck, arms crossed like he'd just finished watching a particularly juicy soap opera.

He whistled. "That was some performance."

Amelia sighed, dragging a hand down her face. "You saw that, huh?"

Kev shook his head and pushed off the truck, strolling closer with the weary amusement of someone who had lived to tell the tale. "Didn't have to. You can feel the drama from across the lot."

He approached the service window, resting an elbow on the ledge. "That woman's been on a rampage lately. She came by last week, ordered my garlic parmesan fries, and then had the audacity to tell me they were—" He twisted his face, affecting a sharp-edged imitation of Evelyn's tone, "'Too garlicky.'"

Beatrice snorted. "They're *garlic parmesan fries.* What did she expect? Hints of mint?"

"Exactly!" Kev threw up his hands. "So I offered her some plain fries instead, trying to be decent, and she looked at me like I'd insulted her. Then she demanded a refund, said she'd 'destroy my reputation,' and stormed off." He let out a dry chuckle, shaking his head.

Amelia exhaled slowly, leaning against the counter. "Great. So now she's coming for The Pink Cupcake."

Kev gave her a sympathetic wince, but his usual breezy tone had a layer of sincerity beneath it. "Yeah. She's making her rounds." His gaze lingered on Amelia for a beat longer, his smirk fading into something more serious. "You want my advice?"

Amelia arched an eyebrow. "Oh, please. Enlighten me."

Kev leaned in slightly, voice low. "Don't give her the satisfaction of a fight. She *lives* for it. It's like oxygen for people like her."

Beatrice, ever the queen of dry commentary, muttered, "She's like a chaos gremlin. If you feed her after midnight, she multiplies."

Kev pointed in agreement. "Exactly that. She doesn't want a refund. She wants to be right, publicly and loudly."

Lila sighed and ran a hand down her ponytail. "Let's just hope she gets bored and moves on. Sooner rather than later."

Amelia wanted to agree. She wanted to believe that this was a one-time tantrum, a little storm of manufactured outrage that would pass like bad weather.

But Amelia felt a chill settle in her stomach. Evelyn wasn't going to move on. She was just getting started.

CHAPTER THREE

THE NEXT MORNING, Amelia arrived at The Pink Cupcake armed with a fresh cup of coffee in one hand and a stubborn sense of determination in the other.

She'd spent most of the night tossing and turning, her thoughts tangled in buttercream and indignation. Part of her had hoped, naively, that Evelyn Waters, after getting whatever twisted satisfaction she'd been looking for, would have moved on. That she'd have found a new victim, maybe a poor unsuspecting barista or an organic juice vendor to harass with her particular brand of high-pitched outrage.

But Amelia knew better. People like Evelyn didn't let things go. They didn't wake up with perspective. They didn't take deep breaths and move on. They didn't meditate, reflect, or call their therapist.

They escalated. They schemed. And judging by the sinking feeling in Amelia's gut, today was going to prove that point.

Her suspicions were confirmed after the lunchtime rush, when Henrietta from Heavenly Soul Food appeared at the service window, waving her phone at them.

"You guys are *trending*," Henrietta announced, her eyes wide with alarm and disbelief.

Amelia blinked. "Trending? That sounds vaguely terrifying."

"Oh, it is," Mina chimed in, appearing just behind Henrietta with a grimace. "Definitely not the good kind."

She held up her phone and spun the screen around like it was evidence in a high-stakes cupcake trial.

A massive, bold headline leapt off the screen:

"AVOID AT ALL COSTS! THE PINK CUPCAKE MADE ME SICK!"

Amelia's stomach dropped.

She took the phone, already bracing herself. The

post was long. An entire novella of melodramatic complaint. The author, clearly Evelyn, had pulled out all the stops. She'd described her "ordeal" in graphic detail, from the "suspicious frosting texture" to the "sudden digestive betrayal." There were ellipses, exclamation marks, and a deeply unnecessary metaphor about "waging war against her insides."

Of course it was Evelyn. And worse, the post had been shared. A lot.

Henrietta leaned her elbows on the truck's counter, watching Amelia's reaction carefully. "It's already blowing up. I saw it reposted on two different neighborhood groups."

Amelia scrolled down to the comments, dreading what she'd find. The top ones weren't encouraging.

"OMG, so sorry this happened to you! I've heard bad things about that place before!"

"Another small business cutting corners, I bet."

"I'm never eating there again. I have a sensitive stomach!"

Amelia groaned and rubbed her temple. "Oh, come *on*."

Mina frowned sympathetically. "It's ridiculous. And she's clearly being dramatic. But you know how these things work. All it takes is one loud voice and a few people ready to jump on a bandwagon."

Henrietta nodded. "Some folks are defending you, don't worry. Regulars are posting pictures of their cupcakes, saying they feel fine. But the comments arguing with Evelyn, she's already responding to all of them. Loudly."

"Perfect," Amelia muttered.

The post continued, a wall of dramatics and frosted vengeance, and even though Amelia knew it was pure fiction, the way people were eating it up made her stomach churn.

"We have standards," she said, her voice edged with frustration. "We check our ingredients. We document everything."

"She *wants* people to panic," Mina said. "She's not trying to get a refund. She's trying to hurt you."

"And she's lying through her teeth." Amelia sighed.

Lila, who had been quietly listening while sipping her coffee, finally broke her silence. "Of *course* she's lying. But arguing with people on the internet is like yelling at a tornado." She gave a half-shrug, like she'd learned this the hard way. "It's not gonna change direction just because you're mad at it."

Amelia let out a sharp exhale, pressing her fingertips to her temples. "So, what, I just do nothing?"

Henrietta, still holding her phone in one hand, gave a thoughtful nod. "The worst thing you can do is engage."

Amelia turned on her heel, her frustration bubbling over. "I can't just let her get away with this."

"I get it," Henrietta said gently. "I do. But trust me, I've seen this play out before. Businesses ruin themselves when they try to fight these things publicly. They get pulled into the drama. Customers lose confidence either way. The mess sticks."

Lila nodded slowly, setting her mug on the counter with a quiet clink. "She's right. If you post something, it needs to be calm, professional, and boring. Evelyn wants a reaction. If you rant, she wins. If you stay measured, she's got nothing to feed off."

Amelia crossed her arms, lips pursed, her thoughts racing. If she stayed silent, Evelyn's post might snowball. The comments would fester. The rumor could grow legs, sprout wings, and fly. But if she struck back, she'd be stepping right onto the stage Evelyn had built for her.

Henritta had the same idea. "You could post something factual. Short. Polite. Remind folks you follow strict safety standards. Reassure your loyal customers without even mentioning Evelyn's name." She paused, then added with a knowing look, "But the second you call her a liar, she'll cry foul and paint herself as the victim. And people *love* a victim."

Lila let out a dry huff of laughter. "She'll put up a new post by lunchtime with a dramatic selfie and a caption like 'bullied for telling the truth.' You know the type."

Amelia clenched her jaw, staring out the window at the lot beyond. The other food trucks bustled in their usual rhythms—laughter, music, fryer sizzles, coffee steam hissing in the distance. But here in her pink pastel world, everything felt off-kilter.

"So, I just let her drag my name through the mud?" she asked quietly, as much to herself as to the others.

Henrietta chuckled under her breath, but it wasn't unkind. "Sometimes the best way to fight fire is to let it burn itself out."

Amelia's fingers itched for her phone, the temptation to type out a scathing rebuttal sitting right behind her teeth. She wanted to call Evelyn out, to defend her team, her work, her reputation.

But she also knew the internet didn't care about nuance. It cared about spectacle.

She drew in a long breath, holding it for a moment before releasing it slowly.

"Fine," she muttered. "No engagement. But if she keeps pushing this..." Amelia's gaze hardened. "I'm not just going to sit back and let her destroy everything we've built."

Henrietta gave Amelia an approving nod. "That's fair. But for what it's worth, I don't think this is going to hurt you long-term. You've got loyal customers. People who know you. And most folks around here already know exactly what Evelyn's like."

Lila leaned against the counter, arms crossed, letting out a slow sigh. "Yeah, this isn't her first stunt. And it won't be the last. She's like a one-woman community theater troupe, and every week is a new performance."

Henrietta snorted, clearly amused. "Exactly. It's not like she's walking around with a sterling reputation. Didn't she threaten to sue one of the sandwich places last month?"

Lila made a face like she'd just remembered a very specific trauma. "Yep. Said her sub had 'too many pickles.' Claimed it threw off her sodium balance or something."

"And she caused a scene at Curry Express a couple weeks ago," Mina added, shaking her head. "Swore the rice was expired. I had to comp her meal just to get her out of the way so the line could move again."

From the back, Beatrice, who had been quietly stirring a bowl of batter with intensity, let out an exaggerated sigh. "Sounds about right. I was in a cafe two weeks ago and she asked for a sugar-free but also extra sweet scone."

Amelia let out a breath, slow, steady, somewhere between exhaustion and bemused disbelief. Just as she opened her mouth to respond, the unmistakable crunch of sneakers on gravel made her stick her head out the window.

Meg and Adam were walking up, both eating burritos. Meg was mid-chew, but her eyes were already sparkling with mischief.

"Hey, Mom," she said after swallowing. "Are you famous now?"

Amelia blinked. "What?"

Adam smirked like he'd been waiting for this moment all morning. "Everyone at school's talking about it. Some lady's going around saying your cupcakes almost killed her."

Amelia groaned, dragging a hand down her face. "Oh, for the love of—"

Meg waved dismissively, her ponytail bobbing. "Relax. It's mostly just gossip. No one's actually worried. Everyone knows Evelyn's a drama queen."

Adam nodded. "Some kid said his mom was in line behind her during the whole cupcake meltdown yesterday. According to him, the only thing that looked 'deathly ill' was Evelyn's attitude."

Beatrice barked a laugh. "That kid's got a good head on his shoulders."

Henrietta grinned. "Smart boy. He should give a TED Talk to half the town."

Amelia shook her head, but she couldn't help the smile tugging at the corners of her mouth. "Well, I hope you're all right. I'd rather not have a social media circus hovering over The Pink Cupcake."

Meg finished the last bite of her burrito and crumpled the paper into a tight little ball. "Then don't give it your energy. Just keep doing what you do, Mom. You're good at it. People see that."

Amelia let her shoulders ease down a little, her fingers finally unclenching from the edge of the counter. Maybe Meg was right. Maybe the best defense wasn't a public battle, but consistency and integrity.

Still, as she glanced back at Henrietta's phone in her hand, she couldn't shake that lingering unease. Evelyn's post was spreading, and fast. She wasn't going to let Evelyn Waters ruin her business.

CHAPTER FOUR

AMELIA HAD BARELY STEPPED out of the shower when she heard the front door creak open downstairs.

At first, it didn't register. She was still wrapped in the lavender-scented haze of shampoo and steam, her mind adrift in the sleepy contentment of hot water and lather. But then came the sound.

Thunk. Thunk. Thunk.

Dan's familiar footsteps echoed through the house. Only they didn't sound quite right. They were quicker than usual. Sharper and not his steady, measured stride. These were clipped, uneven, and urgent, like his feet were moving faster than his thoughts could keep up.

Then came the clatter. A sharp, metallic noise

that rang out in the silence like an alarm. His keys. They hit the kitchen counter with a jarring clang. Not in the little ceramic dish by the fruit bowl, where they always landed with a soft clink. Not with that small, habitual care he showed even when he was tired.

They were dropped carelessly and abruptly. It was such a small detail, a sound most people wouldn't even notice, but it sent a jolt straight through Amelia's chest. Something was wrong.

Still wrapped in her towel, her damp hair twisted into a loose, dripping turban, she stepped carefully onto the hardwood floor, water trailing down her arms and legs like thin silver threads. Her heart was already picking up pace, each beat louder than the last.

She padded down the stairs, barefoot and quiet, each step sinking her deeper into a sense of dread she couldn't yet explain. The warmth from the shower still clung to her skin, but it wasn't enough to stop the chill crawling up her spine.

By the time she reached the kitchen, Dan was already there. He stood by the counter, arms folded tightly across his chest. His shoulders were squared, posture rigid. His brow was furrowed with a tight, concentrated tension she hadn't seen in weeks, maybe months. It was the kind of look she remembered from his worst cases. The kind of look that came with bad news.

She stopped just short of the doorway, one hand braced on the frame for support. Her other hand clutched the edge of her towel a little tighter.

"You're home early," she said.

Dan didn't answer right away. He stood there, completely still for a moment. Then he exhaled and rubbed a hand down his face.

"There's been a death," he said.

Her skin prickled despite the steam still lingering on her body. She took a small step forward, her voice tight and cautious.

"Okay..." she said slowly. "And?"

Dan lifted his eyes. This time, they met hers. They looked serious.

"It's Evelyn Waters."

The name landed like a stone in Amelia's chest. Her knees bent slightly as if her body was preparing to absorb the shock.

"Wait—what?"

Dan's jaw clenched. "She was found dead in the parking lot behind the Gary Community Center," he said. "Someone thought she was asleep in her car. Called it in this morning."

Amelia's hands gripped the back of the nearest dining chair, white-knuckled. Everything around her, the brightness of the kitchen, the faint scent of lemon soap in the air, suddenly felt too sharp.

"Are you serious?"

Dan nodded. "The police responded. She was slumped in the driver's seat, keys still in the ignition. Windows rolled up. No visible injuries. No struggle." He paused. "But she was already gone when they got there."

Amelia's fingers tightened on the chair back. The silence between them stretched long and heavy.

"How?" she finally asked, her voice barely audible.

"They think it was poison."

A dozen thoughts slammed into her brain at once. Poisoning meant investigation. It meant police and questions and evidence. It meant autopsy reports and toxicology screens. It meant the kind of headlines that didn't just vanish after a few days.

It also meant suspects. And Evelyn had just stood in front of a crowd and very publicly accused The Pink Cupcake of making her sick. Had raised her voice. Pointed fingers. Practically issued a threat, right there at the window, with a ruined cupcake and a purse full of drama.

Amelia could feel her thoughts spiraling, skipping steps, jumping to conclusions faster than her logic could catch up.

Was this real? Could Evelyn have actually been poisoned? And was the killer trying to pin this on *her*?

That idea rooted itself fast. She tried to shake it off, to force it away with logic, but fear didn't care about facts. Fear whispered *what ifs* and refused to shut up.

Before she could follow that thread to the end, a sharp knock at the front door made her jump. The sound rang out through the house.

Dan was already moving. She watched him cross the room as she turned and bolted upstairs, dripping water onto the hardwood with each step. She moved on instinct, grabbing the first clothes she saw—sweatpants, a sweatshirt—and twisted her damp hair into something resembling presentable.

By the time she made it back downstairs, Dan had already opened the door.

Detective Walter Hobbs stood in their living room, his presence filling the space like a storm cloud. Tall, stiff-backed, and wearing a coat that looked like it had seen decades of bad news, he didn't smile.

"Hope you two are adjusting to married life," Hobbs said, his tone bone-dry.

Dan stayed behind him, arms folded, watching Amelia carefully.

Amelia crossed the threshold into the living room, arms folded. She sighed, already bracing herself. "I take it you're here about Evelyn?"

Hobbs nodded slowly. His expression was unreadable, but his eyes were sharp. He was already cataloging the room, reading her posture.

"She didn't just keel over," he said. "Preliminary findings suggest poison."

He watched her closely, scanning for tells. Amelia didn't give him one. But her pulse was pounding hard enough in her throat that she was sure Dan could hear it.

"And wouldn't you know it?" Hobbs added, just a touch too casual. "She made quite the scene at The Pink Cupcake yesterday."

Amelia felt her stomach twist. That whole encounter with Evelyn was still vivid.

"She didn't even eat anything from my truck," Amelia said quickly, the words spilling out before she could weigh them. "She came to yell about a cupcake she bought days ago. She didn't order anything new. Didn't taste a thing. She just came to stir the pot."

Hobbs gave a noncommittal shrug, pulling a pen from the inside of his coat and tapping it lightly against a small notepad.

"Doesn't matter," he said. "The public doesn't care about when she ate it. All they'll hear is: 'Woman claims a cupcake made her sick'... and then 'Woman found dead.'"

Amelia clenched her jaw. The weight of that implication pressed down hard. She could already imagine the comments, the headlines, the smug people online who always had something to say.

"This is absurd," she muttered. "I didn't even see her eat anything. She showed up, made a scene, and left. That's it."

Hobbs sighed and pulled out his notepad with the practiced rhythm of a man who'd done this a thousand times. He flipped it open with one hand and clicked his pen with the other, the sound loud in the quiet room.

"Relax," he said. "I'm not here to slap cuffs on you. But I do need to ask a few questions."

He looked up, pen ready. Amelia sat down slowly, her breath finally beginning to settle, but only just. She knew the drill.

"Did you see her eat or drink anything else while she was at Food Truck Alley?"

Amelia frowned, her eyes drifting slightly as her mind tried to rewind. The whole thing had happened so fast. Evelyn's shrill voice had sliced through the buzz of the lunch crowd, her accusations ringing out with enough force to stop conversations mid-sentence. People had turned to watch, cupcakes in hand, some still mid-bite. A few had frozen in place like deer caught in headlights, unsure whether to stay in line or back away slowly.

Had Evelyn eaten anything else? Had she stopped at another truck? Amelia racked her brain.

"It all happened so fast," she said slowly, her brow tightening as she spoke. "She came up to the window with a half-eaten cupcake, yelled at us for a good few minutes, and then stormed off."

She paused, crossing her arms without thinking, fingers tucking into the crook of her elbows. She was trying to mentally replay the scene from start to finish, like scrubbing through grainy security footage in her mind.

"She didn't linger," she added after a moment. "And she definitely wasn't eating anything else while she was with us. But..."

Her gaze unfocused for a second as she tried to

picture the surrounding trucks. The familiar sights of Kev's Fry Shack, Mina's Curry Express, Big Brad's BBQ. Could Evelyn have gone to one of them afterward?

"Maybe she stopped at another truck?" she offered, her voice tinged with doubt. "I didn't see it, but that doesn't mean it didn't happen."

Dan, who had been leaning quietly against the kitchen doorway, straightened slightly. His eyes flicked to Hobbs, then back to Amelia. He didn't say anything, but his jaw was set.

Hobbs nodded, jotting something down with his pen, his hand moving in practiced strokes. His eyes never fully left her, though. He finished the note with a quick tap of the pen against the page, then looked up again. This time, his expression was less clinical. Not quite soft, but calmer. Less interrogative.

"Look," he said, his voice lowering a notch, "I don't think you poisoned the woman."

Amelia blinked. She hadn't realized she'd been holding her breath until she let it out in a long, shaky exhale. Relief fluttered in her chest for a moment, but it didn't last.

"But," Hobbs said, the word landing like a weight on the kitchen floor, "I do think you're about to have a PR nightmare on your hands."

Amelia's relief snapped off like a light switch. The air felt colder again. Her shoulders tensed.

"Excuse me?" she asked, a touch sharper than she meant it.

"If I were you," Hobbs said, slipping his notepad back into his coat pocket, "I'd brace for impact. People remember headlines, not footnotes."

He met her gaze head-on, not unkind, but unflinching.

"And the headline right now is Evelyn Waters claimed your cupcakes made her sick. And now she's dead."

He didn't say it with cruelty. He said it like a detective who'd seen how stories twisted, how public perception warped truth until it no longer mattered. His voice held no malice, just the kind of experience that made you stop pretending things were fair.

With that, he gave a nod, and turned toward the front door.

Dan stepped aside to let him pass, but his eyes stayed locked on Amelia. Hobbs's footsteps echoed down the hallway, steady and final, and then the soft click of the door closing behind him cut through the silence.

It was quiet again. Amelia remained frozen for a

moment. Her fingers rose to her temple, pressing in as though she could physically push the stress out of her head. But the pressure in her chest didn't move. It just pulsed, heavier by the second.

Dan walked over to her and didn't say anything at first. He just slipped an arm around her shoulders and pulled her in. She didn't resist. She leaned against him, her head resting against the soft cotton of his shirt and his warm presence warm.

He pressed a kiss to the top of her damp hair. "We'll get through this."

Amelia closed her eyes. For a few seconds, she let herself believe it. She let herself exist in that quiet moment, in the feel of his arms around her, in the steadiness of his breath against her temple.

She pulled back gently, just enough to look up at him. Even if she didn't say it out loud, she already knew what she had to do.

Evelyn hadn't been poisoned by anything that came from her kitchen. Of that, Amelia was certain. She knew every ounce of batter that went through those ovens, every ingredient that came off the truck. If something had gone wrong, she would have known.

Someone else had poisoned Evelyn. Someone

who had a reason to make her death look like a freak incident, or worse, frame someone else for it.

Amelia wasn't about to sit back and hope it all blew over. Not when her name, and her business, were hanging in the balance. She was going to get to the bottom of this. She was going to find out exactly who wanted Evelyn Waters dead, and why.

CHAPTER FIVE

"BRACE FOR IMPACT."

Detective Hobbs' voice echoed in Amelia's head, a phrase she couldn't seem to shake no matter how many times she told herself to stay calm. It had haunted her all morning, as she made the short drive to Maggie's Diner. Now, as she slid into a cracked vinyl booth near the back, the words settled back into place, right behind her temples, pulsing quietly with each heartbeat.

The seat let out a tired groan beneath her, the kind only well-worn diners could make. She smoothed the laminated menu in front of her, mostly out of habit. It was already curling at the edges from years of syrup-sticky hands and cheap coffee stains. She pretended to study the breakfast specials like she was weighing her options between scrambled eggs and pancakes, but her eyes never really focused on the words.

She wasn't here for the food. She was here for Graham Waters.

It hadn't taken much digging to find him, a little digital sleuthing. Evelyn Waters had never exactly been quiet online. Her social media presence was loud, frequent, and inflammatory, a living scrapbook of complaints. She posted like it was her job: furious Google reviews of hair salons, dramatic updates about "shady" boutique owners, long-winded rants about how the town was full of crooks and incompetents. No detail was too small to become public content.

But when it came to her husband, Evelyn's feed was conspicuously quiet. There were no anniversary tributes, no vacation photos, not even one of those blurry couple selfies from across a restaurant table. She hadn't tagged him in posts celebrating their life together because she hadn't posted about their life together at all. Not even a sarcastic "Happy Birthday to the man who forgot to pick up milk again."

The only time his name surfaced on her page at all was buried in a six-month-old rant about a dispute with their landlord.

"We've been good tenants for YEARS, and now they pull THIS? Absolute vultures preying on hard-working people!"

She'd tagged him at the end of the post, like a footnote in her outrage.

The comments poured in: friends and strangers offering sympathy, advice, or hot takes. But Graham had shared nothing. Not even a like.

That silence told Amelia everything she needed to know. Evelyn was the one who dominated the spotlight and controlled the narrative. She'd curated her online life to be about Evelyn and Evelyn alone. Now she was gone.

On Graham's own page, his tagged locations and regular check-ins had painted a pattern. He wasn't the type to spend mornings at trendy brunch cafés or overpriced juice bars. No, he was more of a Maggie's Diner kind of man. A no-frills greasy spoon on the edge of town where the coffee was strong, the toast was dry, and nobody asked too many questions. And Maggie's had barely changed in thirty years. The air smelled permanently of bacon grease, the windows streaked with fog no matter the season. A neon "Open" sign blinked endlessly in the corner window, stubbornly resisting replacement.

According to what Amelia could piece together,

he came here at least three times a week. Whether it was affordability, routine, or just the comfort of a bottomless mug of coffee and no one bothering to ask how he was doing, she didn't know. But she'd bet on him showing up here today.

And she'd been right.

At the far end of the diner, Graham sat slouched low in his seat. His posture looked like it hadn't changed in hours. He hunched over a chipped plate of dry toast and a cup of black coffee that had likely gone cold fifteen minutes ago.

He looked... wrecked. His clothes were wrinkled, his eyes bloodshot, his shoulders sagging under a weight that no one could name out loud. This was not the image of a grieving husband sobbing into his eggs. But it wasn't the image of a man who had moved on either. It was someone left behind. His eyes weren't focused on anything in particular, just fixed somewhere in the middle distance like he was trying to remember something long lost or forget something too fresh.

Amelia watched him from across the room for a beat longer. She inhaled slowly, letting the breath settle in her lungs. The kind of breath she'd mastered after years in customer service, before delivering hard truths or stepping into tension she couldn't predict. Only this wasn't a bakery dispute or a disgruntled bride demanding lavender frosting at the last minute. This was facing a man whose wife had been found dead.

She had faced angrier men before. Guiltier ones. The kind who leaned too far forward when they talked, whose voices were always just a little too loud. She had looked into the eyes of people who had something to hide and didn't want it found.

But Graham wasn't angry. He wasn't even guarded in the usual way. He was not fearsome. Just hollowed out.

Still, as she stepped forward, Amelia pulled herself into composure. Every movement deliberate. She set her shoulders back and relaxed her brow. She walked with the kind of calm that said she wasn't a threat, but she wasn't to be underestimated either.

She approached the booth and stopped just at the edge, watching for a reaction. Graham didn't look up. Not even a twitch.

She slid into the seat across from him. The silence stretched between them. She waited a moment, then broke it with a voice carefully balanced between professional and warm.

"I hope you don't mind," Amelia said, folding her

hands neatly on the table. Her tone was calm, pleasant. "I thought we should talk."

His jaw shifted, a subtle clench like he was grinding something between his teeth. His eyes flicked up, meeting hers for a fraction of a second before dropping again. But she caught it, the flicker, a flash of something sharp. As if her presence had confirmed something he'd been dreading. Annoyance? Suspicion? Something close to fear. Or maybe anger.

Then, like a reflex, he straightened just enough to look presentable. He forced a polite expression onto his face, mouth flattened into something that might pass for a smile from a distance, but not from this close.

"I don't know you," he said, his voice flat.

Amelia tilted her head slightly, her tone calm but purposeful. "Amelia Walishovsky. I own The Pink Cupcake. The same place your wife said made her sick. The day before she was found dead."

That made him flinch. It was subtle, but it was there. His fingers tightened around his coffee cup, the tips of his knuckles fading a shade lighter. He didn't look away, though. He held her gaze, and when he spoke, his voice was tight and controlled.

"I don't see how that's my problem."

Amelia didn't react right away. She just watched him.

"You don't seem very... surprised," she said softly. "Or upset."

He looked up at her then, really looked. His eyes met hers without blinking. And in them, she didn't see the haze of grief or the dazed weight of someone recently widowed. What she saw was something far more lucid. His eyes were alert, watching her carefully. Thinking. Calculating. Not the look of a grieving husband. More like someone solving a problem with a high-stakes answer.

Amelia felt her own pulse sharpen.

"What exactly do you want, Mrs. Walishovsky?" he asked, his voice lower now. "Why are you here?"

She leaned forward just slightly. Her tone didn't waver. "I'd like to find out some information."

Graham exhaled slowly through his nose. He set his mug down with a dull thud, the ceramic hitting the table like punctuation. His shoulders dropped slightly, the first real sign of something cracking underneath. His hands slid away from the cup and curled around the table's edge, like he needed the feel of something solid beneath his fingertips, something grounding.

"Fine," he muttered. "You want the truth?"

"I do," she said, her voice steady.

His lips parted, then closed again like he was sifting through the versions of the story in his head. He seemed to be trying to decide which one she deserved to hear.

When he finally spoke, his voice was low. "I barely knew my wife anymore."

Amelia didn't blink.

"Anymore?" she prompted gently.

Graham let out a brittle laugh.

"The woman I married..." He shook his head slightly. "She was difficult. Even back then. But at least she was honest about it. She had fire. She could be intense. But she didn't lie the way she did in the end. She didn't... manipulate."

His gaze dropped to his hands again, like he was searching them for answers.

"She changed?" Amelia asked.

Graham nodded. "Bit by bit. By the time we moved to this town, she wasn't interested in fixing things. She didn't want a marriage. She wanted an audience. Evelyn and I were—" he waved a hand loosely in the air. "What's the polite way to put it? 'Estranged but living together'?" One corner of his mouth curled upward, but there was no humor in it.

"She had her life. I had mine. I was sleeping on the couch for months."

"And yet, you were still married," Amelia said.

Graham's hand lifted slowly to his temple, and he pressed his fingertips into the skin.

"She wouldn't agree to a divorce." His voice had gone quiet, nearly swallowed by the low hum of the diner's ancient ceiling fan. "Not unless I paid her more money than I've seen in the last ten years."

Amelia's brow arched slightly. "So you were broke?"

Graham let out a dry snort. "More than broke. Ruined."

He leaned back slightly, the vinyl seat creaking under him. His fingers dragged across the table like they were trying to leave marks behind. "Evelyn's scams didn't just hit strangers. She bled me dry, too. Every time she got a payout, she spent it just as fast."

He shook his head slowly, as if still trying to make sense of it himself.

"Designer handbags. Facials. Spa days. Useless junk. Stuff we had no business affording. She lived like we were royalty, and I was the court jester paying the bill."

He rubbed the back of his neck and sighed.

"I wasn't allowed to touch her money," he said,

and this time the bitterness crept back into his voice. "But she had no problem taking mine. We were behind on everything. Rent, utilities, credit cards. I couldn't keep up. We were drowning in debt. And she didn't care. As long as she got what she wanted."

Amelia didn't speak. She let the silence do the work.

Graham didn't look at her. He just stared at the table, shoulders hunched, hands unmoving.

Evelyn hadn't been running a scam to build a future. She wasn't storing it all away for something bigger. She was spending it the second it came in, using it to live large and leave chaos in her wake. There were no savings, no safety net, no hidden nest egg tucked into a forgotten account. She'd burned through everything she touched.

Which meant if someone had killed her, it wasn't to inherit a fortune. There wasn't one. So what had they killed her for? Not money. Something else.

She studied Graham carefully.

His face was hard to read. Exhausted, absolutely. Bitter, without a doubt. But guilt was harder to parse. There was no obvious crack in his composure, but there was just something in the way he carried himself that was off, like a man hollowed out by too many years of swallowing frustration and learning how to survive inside silence.

What she could see, plainly, was that he had nothing.

Amelia leaned back slightly in the booth, her body language easing. She let her shoulders relax, let the tension melt out of her limbs. Then, gently, she asked, "Did Evelyn have any enemies?"

The question cracked something open. Graham's laugh was fast and sharp and hollow. It burst out of him like a popped balloon.

"Mrs. Walishovsky," he said, shaking his head as the laughter faded, "my wife pissed off everyone. Customers, business owners, neighbors. Even her own family stopped calling years ago."

His voice lowered then. "She could charm you in the beginning. She really could. Made you feel like you were the only person in the room. But it never lasted. She always wanted something. And when she didn't get it..."

He didn't finish. He didn't have to. Amelia heard it anyway.

When she didn't get what she wanted, she punished people. Turned charm into weapons. Threats into performance. She made people pay.

Graham lifted the coffee again, but he didn't

drink. Just held it close, like the warmth might thaw the part of him that still cared.

Then, suddenly, he gripped the mug tighter, his fingers whitening around it.

"I didn't kill her."

The words shot out too fast. Like they'd been building and burst through a crack in his resolve.

Amelia didn't react. Not with words. She simply watched him.

His face was neutral, steady. But the rest of him was not steady at all.

His shoulders were curled in like he was bracing for a punch. His fingers twitched against the mug. His knee, under the table, had started to bounce in a nervous rhythm she didn't think he was aware of.

Was it guilt? Was it fear? Was it relief, now that he had said it out loud? Amelia couldn't say yet.

CHAPTER SIX

AMELIA SAT at the narrow counter inside The Pink Cupcake, her coffee long since gone cold beside her, untouched. The lunch rush had come and gone, leaving the truck in its usual mid-afternoon lull, a stretch of time that normally felt like a small reward. But today, the peace felt like static.

The air was heavy with the lingering scent of sugar and vanilla, the kind of warmth that usually soothed her nerves. But not today.

She wasn't thinking about buttercream. She wasn't thinking about cupcake liners, or Friday specials, or whether they had enough cream cheese left for another batch of red velvet.

She was thinking about Evelyn Waters. Evelyn, who had stood in this very truck not long before that, yelling about being poisoned. And then actually got poisoned and died. Evelyn, who'd built her life on conflict and, according to Graham, had left behind nothing but debt, bitterness, and a long list of burned bridges.

Amelia leaned forward and rested her elbows on the counter. She'd spent the morning sitting across from Evelyn's husband in a greasy diner, watching him unravel just enough to show his scars. She'd come back from that meeting, tied on her apron, and powered through the lunchtime crowd like nothing had happened. She'd smiled, filled orders, taken compliments on her frosting, and thanked customers with the usual cheer in her voice. But all day, beneath it all, her thoughts had been circling the same dark question.

Who would have wanted Evelyn Waters dead? The list was growing. And the answers, so far, weren't getting any simpler.

Even though Hobbs had said she wasn't a suspect *yet*, Amelia felt like the clock had started ticking. The public wasn't going to wait for evidence. They were going to assume. Gossip would twist into theory, theory into blame. If Amelia didn't get ahead of it, and fast, her business might not survive long enough for the truth to catch up.

The door creaked open, and Lila stepped back into the truck from her break, coffee in one hand and her tablet tucked under her arm. Her expression was sharp. She'd clearly picked up on the tension from a mile away.

Lila settled onto the stool across from Amelia and raised an eyebrow as she set her tablet down with a soft *thud*.

"You've got your 'I'm about to solve a murder' face on."

Amelia let out a slow breath. "Hobbs thinks we're about to get hit with a storm of bad press. And if people start asking questions about Evelyn's last meal... well, we already know where their fingers will point first."

Lila sipped her coffee. "Then it's a good thing I didn't spend my break scrolling cat videos."

She slid her tablet across the counter and leaned in slightly, her voice lowering just enough to match the tone in the room. "I started digging."

Amelia blinked. "Already?"

"I just did a surface sweep. Nothing fancy. I checked her name on a couple of local court docket sites, poked around Google Reviews and a few review platforms, complaint boards, and stuff like that."

Amelia managed a small smile. Of course Lila could run a digital background check in under fifteen minutes.

One glance at the screen and Amelia's eyebrows climbed. A few quick taps later, she let out a low whistle. "Wow. I knew she was dramatic, but this is next-level."

"At least four lawsuits in the past two years," Lila said, sitting back with the confidence of someone who'd just cracked open a fresh conspiracy board. "All aimed at small businesses. I didn't pull any sealed filings or anything, just public case listings and whatever Evelyn put out into the world herself. And believe me, she was *not* shy."

Amelia scrolled through the entries, her stomach tightening with every new headline. A catering company Evelyn accused of giving her food poisoning. A coffee shop where she insisted a barista gave her dairy milk on purpose. A fine-dining seafood restaurant she claimed had "nearly ended her" with undercooked scallops and "unforgivable plating." And a health food store where she alleged that a mislabeled vitamin had "derailed her wellness journey."

"She didn't just complain," Amelia murmured. "She escalated, every single time."

Lila nodded. "Yup. First the meltdown, then the dramatic review, then the legal threat. She knew how to stir things up just enough to cause panic, but not quite enough to get herself into trouble."

Amelia sat back and crossed her arms, the knot in her stomach pulling tighter. "She made enemies. And if I had to guess, more than a few of them probably wanted to see her taken down a peg."

Lila raised her cup in a faux-toast. "Or... taken out entirely."

Amelia didn't smile. "This was her business." She was just now realizing the full scope of what they were dealing with.

Lila met her gaze across the counter. She didn't need to say anything, her eyes said it all. But before she could respond, another voice drifted in.

Beatrice, who had been so quietly tucked at the prep station that Amelia had nearly forgotten she was there, looked up from her novel. The spine of the book was creased, her thumb still marking the page. Her tone was dry, but not surprised.

"They settled every time, didn't they?"

"Pretty much," Lila confirmed, her fingers flying across the tablet as she scrolled through the notes she'd compiled. "From what I can tell, none of the lawsuits ever went to trial. The businesses either paid her off or agreed to a quiet settlement to get her off their backs."

Amelia groaned, dragging a hand down her face until her fingers pressed into her cheeks. "So that was the grift. Pretend to get sick, make a huge scene, and then squeeze people until they pay her to leave them alone."

"Looks that way," Lila said, not looking up from the screen. "She wasn't just difficult. She was strategic." She paused, eyes narrowing slightly. "And guess what else?"

Amelia sat up straighter, a ripple of unease threading through her ribs. "What?"

Lila's smirk held no humor this time. "Evelyn had another case pending."

Beatrice, who had resumed stirring her mixing bowl, froze mid-motion. "Another?"

Lila nodded, eyes still locked on the tablet. "Less than a month ago. Against a catering company. She said she got food poisoning at a wedding reception."

Amelia blew out a breath, her shoulders sagging slightly under the weight of the news. "That's almost identical to what she accused us of."

Beatrice let out a low whistle and shook her head, her earrings catching the light as they swung gently. "She really had it down to a science. Same scam, different target."

Amelia leaned in toward the screen again, her brow furrowing. The catering company Evelyn had gone after looked reputable. Clean branding, polished website, glowing reviews, and a whole page of neatly arranged wedding photos. A solid business. The kind of place that didn't deserve to be caught in a mess like this.

Amelia tapped her fingers lightly on the counter, each tap syncing with the rising tempo of her thoughts.

"And now she's dead," she said softly.

The words lingered in the air, drawing the warmth out of the truck like a breeze had slipped through the door.

For all of Evelyn's chaos, she'd been *here*, just yesterday. Loud, alive, and threatening refunds like it was her life's work. Now there was only silence where her noise used to be.

Beatrice was the one who finally broke it, her voice calm but pointed. "So the real question is, who finally had enough and snapped?"

Lila exhaled through her nose, slow and steady. She closed the tablet and set it down with a soft *thud*, the sound feeling heavier than it should.

"I hate to say it," she murmured, "but that's probably a *long* list."

Amelia nodded slowly, her thoughts already leaping two, three steps ahead. "She didn't just ruin reputations. She went after people's livelihoods. That kind of thing leaves scars. She made enemies."

Beatrice looked down at her mixing bowl, but didn't stir. "And enemies don't always stay quiet."

Amelia drummed her fingers against the countertop, once, twice, then again.

"The real question is..." she said softly, eyes narrowing, "which one had the opportunity to do something about it?"

Lila picked up her tablet again and snapped it shut with a decisive click.

"Well, if I were a detective—" she arched a brow at Amelia, "—I'd start by figuring out who had the most to lose from her latest scam."

Amelia exhaled and nodded, her jaw tightening. "That's a good place to start."

Her eyes drifted back to the catering company's name glowing faintly on the screen. They had motive, they had history with Evelyn, and now, they had Amelia's full attention.

CHAPTER SEVEN

AMELIA PACED BAREFOOT on the hardwood floor. Her sleeves were rolled up, pushed past her elbows, and her hair was twisted into a messy bun. Every time she passed the kitchen table, she caught a different angle of the chaos she'd left there. Notes, printouts, old blog screenshots, yellow sticky notes. Plus a to-do list that had started that morning with practical plans ("buy eggs") and descended into full obsession, the scribbled and underlined: "find a motive."

The only light in the room came from her laptop, glowing persistently in the darkened kitchen. It cast long shadows across the paperwork, draping every page in that cool, digital blue. She had really tried to step away from it all after dinner. She'd even stood in the doorway of the living room, half-considering a sitcom rerun or a second slice of apple pie. But her brain refused to let go.

Her conversation with Graham that morning played on a loop in her mind. Something was off. And it had set her thoughts circling like buzzards. Now, those thoughts had zeroed in on another name: Kimberly Reeves.

Reeves & Co. Catering wasn't just some hole-in-the-wall Evelyn could shake down for a quick settlement. This wasn't a local cupcake truck she could threaten with bad reviews. This was a sleek, polished, high-end operation with menus printed on letterpress stock, hors d'oeuvres with ingredients Amelia had to Google just to understand, and a reputation so carefully curated it practically sparkled.

Amelia leaned over the laptop again, her fingers tapping the arrow key with just a little more force than necessary. The lawsuit summary popped back up:

Waters v. Reeves & Co.

Filed three weeks ago. Then it was just dropped, without a legal response, social media damage control, or a polished, lawyer-written statement denying all wrongdoing on Kimberly's part. Just silence.

Amelia clicked over to another tab: a collage of social media snippets, local news screenshots, and fundraiser photos, all tied to the gala Evelyn had cited in her complaint. It had been a children's literacy fundraiser, hosted at a historic mansion with state senators, ribbon-cuttings, and a dessert bar that had made the local lifestyle magazine's "Ten Must-Try Bites" list.

This was the kind of gala where appearances mattered. where any disruption, especially one involving food, would have caused a splash. A complaint from a guest like Evelyn, known for her theatrics, would've gotten attention.

And yet, she hadn't gone public. Instead, Evelyn had done something unusual for her. She just filed a lawsuit, and then dropped it. Why?

Amelia pulled up a screenshot she'd saved from an old forum archive, a post from Evelyn that had long since been deleted. It looked innocuous at first glance, just a vague comment about "food safety standards" and "being fed lies on silver trays."

But the caption was smug. And just subtle enough to be missed for what it really was. Not a complaint, but a warning.

Amelia leaned in closer to the screen. This wasn't about being sick from a canapé. Again, it was about control.

"Some people think they can serve whatever they want and hide behind fancy menus. But I've seen the kitchen. I know the truth. One day, everyone else will, too."

A threat slipped into the comment section like a blade hidden in a linen napkin. Not a single accusation spelled out, but every word loaded. Amelia stared at the screen for another long moment. She could almost hear Evelyn's voice in her head, sly and smug. Someone who always wanted the last word, even if it came after she was gone.

Then Amelia pushed away from the table. She didn't need one more half-formed idea to keep her awake. She needed answers.

Kimberly Reeves was the last name in Evelyn's long list of legal sparring partners, and maybe the one who mattered most.

Amelia crossed the room with purpose, footsteps silent but steady. The air in the kitchen felt heavier now, like the walls themselves had leaned in to listen. Kimberly hadn't fought the lawsuit. She hadn't dismissed it, denied it, or defended herself, not in court, not in the press, not anywhere.

Because she couldn't. Or maybe because she wouldn't.

Maybe Evelyn just filed a legal complaint to send a message. Wrapped in formal language, obscured by legalese and line items for damages, but beneath it all, it was something else entirely. A warning? A threat? Blackmail?

She stood there, motionless for a moment. Then came the soft sound of footsteps down the hall, familiar and warm. She didn't turn. She knew the rhythm by heart.

Dan appeared in the doorway, rubbing the back of his neck, his expression still hazy from sleep but edged with quiet awareness, the kind only years of late-night cases and early-morning instinct could forge.

His gaze swept across the scene to her laptop, still glowing; the notes, spread like breadcrumbs across the table; the tea she hadn't touched since pouring it hours ago. And then he looked at her. That same look he always gave her when she was chasing something too hard and too fast, but might just catch it anyway.

"You're still going?" he asked, voice low, rough from sleep.

Amelia turned the laptop toward him and gestured for him to look.

"I think Evelyn was extorting Kimberly Reeves."

Dan stepped closer, narrowing his eyes at the screen.

"The caterer?"

"Yep." She tapped the side of the laptop once, her fingertip sharp against the edge. "Evelyn left breadcrumbs all over the internet. She had something on Kimberly, something big enough to keep her quiet. Maybe Kimberly paid her to drop the lawsuit."

Dan stayed quiet for a moment, his arms folding across his chest in that way he always did when he was fully locked in, thinking like a detective, measuring what she said, balancing what it meant. Amelia watched him, already knowing the wheels were turning.

Finally, he spoke, voice slow and thoughtful. "If you're right, then Kimberly had motive." He paused again, his eyes lifting to meet hers. "And maybe fear."

Amelia nodded slowly. "Exactly. If Evelyn pushed too hard, if she threatened to go public again later on..."

She didn't need to finish the sentence. Dan was already there.

He exhaled through his nose and stepped into the kitchen fully. His hands slid into his pockets, but his eyes never left her. He studied her like he was reading a report.

"You going to talk to her?" he asked.

The decision had already planted itself firmly in her chest. "I have to," she said. "She's the next piece of this puzzle."

Dan didn't argue. He didn't remind her of what could happen. He just watched her with that familiar look of admiration, worry, and reluctant respect. The look of a man who knew exactly who he'd married and loved her too much to try and change it.

Then, gently: "Just be smart about it. Hobbs isn't going to like you stepping on his toes."

Amelia gave a tired but pointed smile. "Then I'll be careful not to leave footprints."

Dan shook his head and chuckled, dry and amused, but also a little helpless. "I didn't just marry a cupcake baker, did I?"

Amelia smirked. "You married a cupcake baker who solves murders before bedtime."

CHAPTER EIGHT

AMELIA TURNED into the parking lot of Reeves & Co. Catering, her fingers tightening around the steering wheel. The building rose in clean lines and frosted glass, strikingly modern against the quieter, older storefronts of the surrounding district. Every inch of it radiated polish and precision.

The moment Amelia stepped through the doors, she was greeted by the hum of high-functioning activity, an elegant sort of chaos.

Staff moved briskly through the sleek, open-concept kitchen and adjoining prep space, their black chef coats pressed and spotless despite the flurry of movement. Some were plating hors d'oeuvres with tweezers and practiced delicacy, others assembling serving trays with near military efficiency. Phones rang softly from a back office, clipboards changed hands, and a courier wheeled in a tower of wine crates without ever breaking the flow.

The air was filled with the scent of roasted rosemary, browned butter, and something savory Amelia couldn't quite name but instantly wanted to eat.

At the far end of the kitchen, a long table had been turned into a mock reception setup: white linen, brushed gold flatware, and crystal stemware lined up with military precision. It was clearly a test run for an upcoming event, and no detail was being left to chance.

This wasn't a kitchen, it was a stage. And Kimberly Reeves was the director. She stood in the center of the action, her presence unmistakable. Barking orders in a crisp tone that somehow cut through the noise without raising her voice. She carried a digital tablet in one hand and a set of tasting spoons in the other, switching between screens and seasoning with a practiced rhythm that could only come from running the show for years.

Amelia had seen her type before, but Kimberly wasn't just a perfectionist. She was a strategist. Every gesture, every word, every raised eyebrow sent ripples through the staff.

And as if she could sense the disruption before it

even reached her, Kimberly turned and spotted Amelia in an instant. Her eyes, sharp, cool blue, narrowed ever so slightly.

Amelia had barely opened her mouth when Kimberly called across the space, voice flat and unamused. "I don't do free tastings."

Amelia almost smiled.

"I'm not here for food," she said smoothly, clasping her hands lightly in front of her. "I'm here to talk about Evelyn Waters."

A hint of something passed over Kimberly's face, then nothing. She masked it like a pro.

Kimberly exhaled slowly, crossed her arms, and shifted her weight.

"So the vultures are already circling," she said, her tone dry enough to scrape.

Amelia tilted her head. "Vultures?"

Kimberly didn't blink. "I assume you're with the press. Or one of those true-crime podcasters. Trying to get your hands on a scandal before someone else does."

"Not exactly," Amelia said, offering her business card across the counter. "I run The Pink Cupcake. Evelyn paid me a visit before she died."

Kimberly took the card but didn't glance at it. Her eyes stayed on Amelia, narrowed now.

"I'm not interested in giving a statement," she said. "And I have nothing to add to whatever story you're telling."

"Good," Amelia said calmly. "Because I'm not telling a story. I'm looking for the truth."

That earned her a pause. Kimberly uncrossed her arms. She let out a dry chuckle. "Let me guess. You want to know if I poisoned her?"

Amelia didn't blink. "Did you?"

Kimberly tossed a pen onto the counter with a flick of her wrist, the clatter of plastic loud against the polished surface. Then she laughed.

"I wish."

Amelia arched an eyebrow.

Kimberly gave her an assessing look, and then turned her back. With brisk, practiced efficiency, she grabbed a clipboard from the nearby counter and began flipping through it as though Amelia were a delivery mix-up she needed to sort before lunch service.

"Evelyn was a menace," she said, not bothering to lower her voice. The words fell like knives: clean, precise, unapologetic.

Amelia caught a flicker of movement from the corner of her eye. One of the catering staff had looked up, instinctively, then just as quickly turned back to the vegetables they were slicing.

"She made her living shaking down businesses," Kimberly continued. "Suing, threatening, dangling whatever fake evidence she could scrape together to get a payout. And when that didn't work, when we didn't play along, she'd go to the press. Smear your name, sabotage your contracts. She didn't need to win. She just needed you to bleed." She snapped the clipboard shut with a sharp *crack*, then turned back toward Amelia, her eyes steely. "That woman nearly ruined me."

Amelia crossed her arms, steady but quiet. "But she didn't."

Kimberly met her gaze without so much as a flinch. "No," she said. "She didn't."

Her voice didn't rise. It was a statement of fact. An iron line drawn in the air between them. Because Kimberly Reeves wasn't the type to lose a fight. She was the type who ended it.

Amelia tilted her head slightly. "Then why did she drop the lawsuit?"

Kimberly's lips twitched into a tight, knowing smirk. "Because she had bigger fish to fry."

Kimberly set the clipboard aside and leaned forward slightly, her elbows resting against the pris-

tine marble edge. Her voice dropped just enough
that the kitchen staff couldn't hear, but it still carried
enough edge to slice butter.

"Evelyn could dig up dirt," she said. "Maybe she
dug up too much."

Amelia raised an eyebrow. "What do you mean?"

Kimberly didn't answer right away. The smirk
that had danced at the corners of her mouth faded.
Her hands stilled.

"She was making enemies," she said finally.
"Real ones. The kind you don't provoke."

"That's not the same as giving me an answer,"
Amelia said calmly.

Kimberly's jaw shifted slightly. A muscle
twitched just below her cheekbone.

"She was threatening the wrong people," she
said. "Blackmailing people she didn't fully understand. People who didn't appreciate their secrets
being tossed around."

Amelia narrowed her eyes. "Who are we talking
about?"

Kimberly's eyes flicked toward the kitchen, then
back. Then, in a voice quieter than before, almost
reluctant, she said:

"City Hall."

The words landed like a dropped plate. Amelia stiffened.

"City Hall?"

That wasn't what Amelia had been expecting.

She'd assumed Evelyn had pushed someone too far, a café owner, a frustrated caterer, someone who'd finally snapped after being threatened with lawsuits and social media attacks.

But this was bigger. Her voice remained calm, but her pulse began to thrum steadily beneath her skin. "What does that mean?"

Kimberly didn't answer right away. Instead, she glanced around. The catering staff were still working, still slicing and plating and prepping trays, but something in their movements had gone taut. No one was eavesdropping. But everyone was aware.

Kimberly's voice, when it came, was quieter now. Lower, but laced with clarity.

"It means Evelyn wasn't just scamming business owners," she said, her gaze fixed on Amelia. "She had her sights on someone in local government. Someone with influence." Her fingers tightened subtly around the edge of the counter. "I can't tell you who," she added, voice clipped.

Amelia's mind surged with possibilities. City

Hall. Of course. It explained the silence around the lawsuit. It explained Evelyn's sudden shift from small, scrappy targets to someone with real power. Someone she should never have gone after.

And maybe, it explained why she was now dead. Because if Evelyn had threatened the wrong person, someone in office, someone with a title, someone with enough reach to make a problem disappear, then she hadn't just crossed a line. She had stepped into a world where consequences were handled quietly and permanently.

Before Amelia could ask anything else, Kimberly straightened. Her spine lengthened. Her hands smoothed over her clipboard. The tension around her eyes smoothed out like a cloth pulled taut over a stain. Her voice returned to its clipped register.

"That's all I'm saying," she said. "Now, if you don't mind, I have a business to run."

It was the kind of dismissal that didn't need emphasis. Amelia could press, but something told her it wouldn't get her anywhere. Not today.

So she nodded once, slowly. "I appreciate your time."

Kimberly offered nothing in return, not even a smile.

Amelia turned and walked toward the front of the building, her heels clicking quietly across the immaculate floors.

The moment she stepped outside, the crisp air bit at her cheeks, but it wasn't enough to ground her. Her thoughts were spinning. Too fast. Too loud.

Kimberly had just confirmed what Amelia had only started to suspect. Evelyn hadn't just been running a con. She'd been holding something over someone important. Someone with enough to lose that they'd rather eliminate a threat than negotiate.

Amelia reached into her bag, fingers brushing past her wallet and notepad before closing around her keys. But just as she reached her car, she stopped short.

Something was wrong. Her breath caught as her gaze dropped to the ground. Both front tires. *Slashed.*

Thick, jagged cuts sliced through the rubber like someone had taken a knife to them and made sure it hurt.

Her heart thudded once, hard, before settling into a cold, rapid rhythm.

This was a message. Someone knew she was asking questions. And they wanted her to stop.

She took a slow step back from the car, her hand

tightening around her keys like they could offer protection.

Then, with deliberate calm, she reached into her coat pocket, pulled out her phone, and tapped the screen. There was only one person she would call.

CHAPTER NINE

"YOU'RE KIDDING ME."

Dan's voice was sharper than usual, tight with concern and barely contained frustration, the kind that only came out when he was one breath away from putting a hole through his desk.

"Someone actually slashed your tires?"

"Yes," Amelia said, the word coming out with a sigh. She already knew exactly where this was going. Her nerves were still crackling, but she kept her tone calm.

"And before you ask, no," she added, cutting him off preemptively. "I didn't see who did it."

On the other end of the line, there was a heavy pause. She could picture him clearly, probably standing in his precinct office, running a hand through his hair with his jaw clenched so tightly it hurt.

"Amelia," he said finally.

"I know," she cut in again. "I know what you're going to say. It was a message. Someone wants me to stop poking around."

Dan didn't answer right away. The silence pressed against her ear like static. Then he spoke, quieter now, but firmer. "That's exactly why I'm saying it. Maybe you should stop."

He didn't say it like a lecture. He said it like a man who had just imagined the worst and was trying not to show how much that scared him.

Amelia had expected it. She didn't blame him. If the roles were reversed, she'd be begging him to stay out of it, too. But she wasn't going to.

"If someone went through the trouble of slashing my tires," she said evenly, "they're scared of what I might find."

Dan sighed again, and this time she heard him sit down, the chair creaking. "I don't like this."

"I know," she said.

"You're still going to keep digging."

It wasn't a question.

A small smile tugged at her lips. "You married me."

Another pause. And then, a reluctant exhale that sounded almost like a laugh.

"If anything else happens," Dan said, voice dropping into firm, unmistakable territory, "you call me immediately. No waiting or downplaying. No 'it's probably nothing.' Understood?"

"Deal," she said.

And she meant that.

The next morning, Amelia was back on the trail. She headed straight to the Gary County Municipal Offices, her breath visible in the brisk air as she stepped out of her car. The building was boxy and beige, the kind of architecture that practically whispered, *Nothing exciting ever happens here.* She doubted that was true.

Inside, the air was too warm, dry from recycled heat and scented faintly with copier toner and whatever had been burned in the office microwave one too many times. The overhead fluorescent lights buzzed with faint menace.

A woman behind the front desk sat typing, her cardigan dotted with cat hair and her expression unreadable. Amelia approached with a clipboard tucked under one arm, a prop more than anything. She offered her most pleasant voice.

"Hi. I was hoping to speak with Jackie Mitchell? Someone told me she handles health inspection records for local businesses."

That wasn't a lie. Not exactly. Jackie's name had surfaced in old threads Evelyn had left behind, comments about overlooked citations, fast-tracked permits, and whispered accusations of bribes in exchange for blind eyes. Evelyn had been vague but persistent.

The receptionist glanced up, her gaze flicking over Amelia, then pointed down the hallway. "Past the vending machines. Third door on the left, if she's in."

Amelia offered a grateful smile. "Thanks so much."

She walked down the corridor, each step padded against the dull industrial carpet. Her fingers tightened slightly on the clipboard. At the third door, she paused. The door was open.

Inside, a tall woman in a fitted slate-gray blazer stood by a filing cabinet, flipping through a thick folder with practiced ease. Her sleek dark hair was clipped back, not a strand out of place.

Jackie Mitchell. Amelia had seen her photo in

council newsletters and business registries, but the real-life version carried more steel than the grainy headshots suggested. She hesitated just a beat, then cleared her throat.

"Jackie Mitchell?"

The woman stiffened, and didn't turn right away. Instead, she finished the page she was scanning, then slowly turned, her sharp brown eyes assessing Amelia with a glance that was all business.

"Yes?" she said. "Who's asking?"

Amelia stepped into the doorway with an easy smile. "Amelia Walishovsky. I run The Pink Cupcake."

Jackie's expression didn't shift much, but recognition flickered behind her eyes.

Amelia continued, still friendly. "I was hoping to ask you about Evelyn Waters."

Jackie blinked once, slowly. "What about her?"

Amelia didn't answer right away. She let the silence stretch just long enough to shift the balance in the room.

"She was found dead two days ago."

The effect was immediate. Jackie's fingers stilled against the folder in her hands. The pages crinkled softly under her grip. And for one unguarded moment, her eyes betrayed something she didn't intend to show. Amelia couldn't tell if it was shock, relief, or something in between.

Then, as if reminding herself she was in a municipal office and not under interrogation lights, Jackie straightened, cleared her throat, and dropped her gaze to the paperwork.

"I saw it on the news," she said.

Amelia tilted her head. "And?"

Jackie shut the folder with a little more force than necessary and placed it down with careful precision.

"And nothing," she said crisply. "I don't know why you're here."

Amelia took a slow step forward, closing the distance by inches rather than confrontation.

"I think you do."

Jackie's jaw tensed. Her lips thinned into a narrow line of irritation. "I don't have time for this."

Her tone was clipped and dismissive. It was clear Jackie Mitchell operated in a world where she was rarely challenged. A woman used to short answers, closed doors, and the assumption that her authority would speak for itself.

But Amelia didn't rattle that easily. She held her ground. "Then I'll make it quick."

She paused, just long enough to make sure Jackie couldn't look away.

"You and Evelyn had a history. She accused you of taking bribes. And recently, she started threatening you again."

Jackie's nostrils flared. A single breath in. Her eyes narrowed, and her arms folded across her chest in a defensive knot.

"That's a lie," she said. The words came out too fast.

Amelia arched a brow. "So she wasn't threatening you?"

The question hung in the air like a challenge.

Jackie exhaled sharply and turned away, dragging a hand through her carefully styled hair that knocked a few strands loose. Her other hand braced against the filing cabinet for a moment as if she needed the grounding.

Her irritation was no longer theoretical. It had weight now.

"Look," she snapped. "Evelyn was a professional troublemaker, okay? She *lived* for drama. She'd blow into a restaurant or bakery, claim she was poisoned by a cupcake or a glass of wine, and the next thing you knew, she was demanding compensation."

Amelia listened silently, noting every shift in

tone, every emphasis. Jackie wasn't lying. But she wasn't telling everything, either.

"She knew how to push people," Jackie continued, her arms still crossed. "And if they didn't fold right away, she'd threaten to report them, fake violations, outdated equipment, imaginary rat droppings. It didn't matter. She'd find a crack and wedge herself into it." Her voice dropped lower, her gaze flicking back toward Amelia. "And she didn't just stop at businesses. She had real dirt on people. *Everyone.*"

Amelia folded her arms slowly, mirroring Jackie's stance, letting the silence stretch just long enough to be uncomfortable.

"Including you?"

Jackie didn't flinch, but her jaw tightened. A flicker of something crossed her face, something closer to calculation. She was deciding, right there in front of Amelia, just how much to say, or how little she could get away with.

The silence that followed was tense enough to press against the walls. One second. Two. Three.

Then Jackie sighed, and something in her posture eased in fatigue. Her shoulders dipped slightly, her hand falling away from her crossed arms to rest on the edge of the desk. The armor didn't drop completely, but there were cracks in it now.

"Evelyn had suspicions about me," Jackie admitted, her voice quieter, more careful. "She didn't have proof. She never *had* proof. But that didn't stop her from acting like she did." She paused, then continued, almost to herself. "She understood something most people don't. Sometimes all you need is the *hint* of a scandal. The suggestion, in the right ear."

Amelia studied her. The tightness in her voice. The way her fingers tapped the desk once, twice, and then stilled.She wasn't a criminal. She was someone who had been cornered. Someone who knew what it felt like to have a noose slowly tighten, even if it never actually closed.

"She made you nervous," Amelia said softly.

Jackie looked away.

"And did Evelyn try to... make some kind of deal with you?"

Jackie let out a sharp, humorless laugh.

"Oh, she *tried*," she said, shaking her head in disbelief, or maybe disbelief that she was admitting it out loud. "She came to my office twice. Started vague hints about 'transparency' and 'protecting the integrity of City Hall.' Then it got more pointed. Said she was considering 'exposing' a few things unless I showed a little... cooperation." Her voice darkened. "I told her exactly where she could stick her threats. I don't negotiate with scammers. I never have. I wasn't about to start with Evelyn Waters."

The conviction in her tone was solid, but it sounded like it was meant to convince the speaker more than the listener.

She tilted her head. "But Evelyn didn't drop it, did she?"

She didn't answer immediately. But she didn't deny it either. Finally, Jackie let out another long breath. Her gaze dropped toward the floor, as if looking directly at Amelia now would be too much.

"No," she said. "She didn't."

The admission lingered. Amelia stood there. In that moment, she understood. Jackie Mitchell had something to hide. Maybe it was sketchy dealings with permits, maybe it was something as simple as a bad decision wrapped in politics, but it wasn't murder.

Jackie hadn't paid Evelyn. She hadn't given in, but she hadn't been able to ignore her either. Evelyn had kept the pressure on, circling like a vulture, threatening exposure, stirring just enough doubt to make Jackie sweat. And Jackie, for all her sharpness and pride, had been left waiting for the fallout. She was no killer. Just another unwilling participant in

Evelyn's game, caught in a mess she hadn't been able to stop, but hadn't fed either.

Amelia stepped back, giving Jackie room to retreat behind her desk. Jackie just nodded once and sat down, the conversation officially closed. Amelia left the office without another word.

Back in the hallway, the building felt colder than when she'd entered. The fluorescent lights buzzed faintly overhead. A maintenance cart squeaked somewhere in the distance.

She had come to City Hall looking for answers. Instead, she'd found another victim.

A dead end. But not a wasted visit. Because now she knew: Evelyn had reached higher than anyone realized. She'd poked and prodded her way up the ladder, throwing accusations like darts, hoping one of them would stick. And somewhere in that process, she'd hit a nerve.

Amelia stepped outside, the wind catching her coat as she descended the concrete steps.

Jackie wasn't the one who'd snapped. Which meant the person who had was still out there. And if they thought a few slashed tires were going to scare her off, they were going to be disappointed.

CHAPTER TEN

AMELIA LEFT the health department building with the familiar feeling of disappointment settling deep in her chest. Jackie Mitchell hadn't given her anything. She had hoped more than she wanted to admit that she would walk away with something. A lead, or at the very least a hint that she was getting warmer. Instead, she was walking away with wind-burned cheeks.

The crisp Oregon air bit harder than she expected as she slid into her car. She slammed the door with more force than necessary, started the engine, and checked the time with a grimace. If she hurried, she could just make it back in time for the tail end of the lunch rush. Back to the cupcakes.

Back to the part of her life that, at least for the next few hours, still made sense.

By the time she pulled into the lot behind The Pink Cupcake, the truck was already surrounded by a small but eager line of customers. Their chatter carried on the breeze, cheerful and oblivious, a strange contrast to the leaden mood still sitting heavily on Amelia's shoulders.

She parked around the back, quickly tied her apron around her waist in a practiced knot, and pushed open the door to step inside.

The kitchen was its own world: warm, bustling, alive with the rhythm of baking and serving. It grounded her, but only just.

Lila stood at the register and handed out orders with a dazzling efficiency that was half cheerleader, half drill sergeant.

"You're back," Lila said. "How'd it go?"

Amelia grabbed a pair of tongs and began refilling the display case. Her voice came out wry and resigned. "It didn't. Jackie Mitchell gave me nothing. Just another dead end."

"I could have told you that," Beatrice called over her shoulder, not missing a beat as she applied a perfect raspberry buttercream swirl. "That woman couldn't tell the truth if it was laminated and triple notarized."

Amelia gave a soft snort as she arranged lemon cupcakes in neat rows. "I didn't say she was lying. I said she was afraid. But she wasn't the one who snapped."

"So," Lila said, stepping aside to let Amelia take the next order, her curiosity obvious, "what now?"

"Now," Amelia said, handing a lemon cupcake to a customer with a practiced smile that barely covered the frustration boiling under the surface, "I work."

The line moved briskly, and Amelia found herself sliding back into the familiar motions: handing out cupcakes, making small talk, offering napkins and warm thank-yous. The kind of muscle memory that made her almost forget for a moment that murder and suspicion were lurking just outside the pink walls of her food truck.

By the time the last customer wandered off and the kitchen finally settled into its usual post-rush lull, Amelia slid onto the stool at the counter and opened her laptop with a sigh. Her body might have been still, but her mind was kicking into overdrive again, running circles around itself.

She tapped her fingers lightly against the counter, thinking out loud. "Who else would want

Evelyn dead? Should I look into Graham a bit more?"

"The husband seems likely," Beatrice said dryly, wiping her hands on her apron without looking up. "If I were married to her, I'd kill her."

Amelia cracked a small smile despite herself. Dark humor was Beatrice's love language.

Lila perked up. "Speaking of, remember my friend Zoe who works at Simcoe Insurance?"

"The one who helped you figure out your car claim?" Amelia asked, her curiosity sharpening.

"Yep. We were chatting about Evelyn's death, and she just casually dropped it. Apparently, Evelyn had taken out a life insurance policy."

Amelia sat up straighter, her interest instantly piqued. "Wait. She had a policy?"

Lila nodded, swirling her coffee absentmindedly. "Yep. Zoe said it got flagged for processing after the police notified the insurer. Standard procedure, I guess, when there's a suspicious death."

Amelia tapped her fingers on the counter, thinking. "So Graham hadn't received a payout yet?"

"Zoe didn't say much," Lila said, digging into the pocket of her jeans for her phone. "Confidentiality rules, you know. But I figure if the policy's under review, then no, he hasn't gotten a dime."

Amelia chewed the inside of her cheek for a second, her mind racing ahead. If Graham wasn't sitting on a sudden windfall, that changed things. Or complicated them even more.

"Can I call her?" Amelia asked.

"She's usually stuck in meetings during the day," Lila said, scrolling through her contacts. She tapped a few times and handed the phone over. "But her secretary's nice. Just say it's about a file. Keep it vague."

Amelia nodded, already stepping toward the door with quick, determined strides. Within seconds, she was outside the truck, the early afternoon wind whipping strands of hair into her face. She hunched her shoulder against the gusts, shielding her phone as she punched in the number Lila had given her.

The line rang twice, then picked up with a clipped, professional voice. "Simcoe Insurance, this is Cassandra."

Amelia tucked a loose strand behind her ear and forced her voice to sound bright and pleasant. "Hi, Cassandra. I'm trying to reach Zoe Anders. It's Amelia Walishovsky."

"Oh! Zoe's out for a site visit right now. Can I take a message?"

"Yes, please." Amelia shifted her weight from

foot to foot, scanning the lot out of habit. "Just let her know I'm a friend of Lila's. I have a question. It's time-sensitive. Could she call me back when she gets a moment?"

"I'll pass it along as soon as she's back in the office," Cassandra promised.

"Thank you." Amelia hung up.

Back inside the truck, she dropped onto the stool beside Lila with more force than she intended.

"She wasn't there," Amelia said shortly. "But I left a message."

Lila nodded, not looking the least bit concerned. "She'll call back. Zoe always does."

At the prep station, Beatrice glanced up from the cupcake she was decorating. "What exactly are you hoping she says?"

Amelia opened her laptop again, tapping the trackpad absently as she stared at the screen. "That Graham was going to get a big payout," she said. "Which would explain why he'd kill his wife."

━━━

After dinner, Amelia loaded the dishwasher while Dan packed up the leftovers, humming quietly under his breath. Adam lingered at the table, absently eating the last crusty edge of garlic bread straight from his plate, crumbs dusting the placemat.

The kitchen was filled with the soft, comforting sounds of ordinary life: dishes clinking, chairs scooting across the tile floor, Meg sighing loudly as she told Adam to please stop humming *for the love of all that is holy*.

It was domestic and warm, exactly the kind of scene Amelia usually loved to sink into at the end of a long day. But not tonight.

Amelia kept sneaking glances at her phone, checking it like she was waiting for a lifeline to drop into her palm. Every buzz of a group text or email notification made her chest clench with expectation and then deflate again.

She had just finished drying her hands and was reaching for her tea mug when the screen lit up across the kitchen counter. Zoe Anders.

Amelia snatched up the phone and stepped into the hallway, tucking herself away from the clatter of dishes and the soft drone of the kids' conversation at the kitchen table. She cradled the phone against her ear and answered quickly.

"Hi, Zoe. Thanks for calling me back."

"Of course," Zoe said warmly. "It sounded important."

"I'm sorry to bother you," Amelia said, already feeling a small prickle of guilt for pulling someone into this mess.

"No worries," Zoe replied with an easy laugh. "Sorry it took me a bit to respond. You said you're Lila's friend?"

"Yes," Amelia said, smiling despite the weight in her chest. "We run The Pink Cupcake together."

"Oh, of course! I've been there." Zoe's tone brightened. "My favorite is still plain chocolate, but I've been meaning to try your other flavors."

Amelia chuckled, the sound easing some of the tightness in her shoulders. "Please do. I'll even sneak you an extra one if you come by."

"I might take you up on that," Zoe said lightly, then her voice shifted back to something more professional, gently prompting, "So, you had a question about life insurance?"

Amelia nodded, even though Zoe couldn't see her. "Well, it's about Evelyn Waters. I understand she had a life insurance policy with your company."

There was a small pause on the other end of the line.

"I have to be careful what I say, of course," Zoe said carefully. "I can't give you official policy information."

"I know," Amelia said quickly. "I'm not asking for anything sensitive. Just..." She hesitated, choosing her words with care. "Did her husband get a huge payout already?"

Another brief silence. Amelia could practically hear Zoe weighing what she could and couldn't reveal.

Then, cautiously, Zoe said, "She did have a policy. A substantial one. But there was something odd."

"Odd how?" she asked.

"The beneficiary was changed recently," Zoe said, her voice lowering slightly, as if leaning closer to the phone might somehow make the conversation more private. "As in, very recently. Just a few weeks before her death."

Amelia felt the breath catch in her throat. Her mind leapt ahead, already racing through implications, possibilities.

"Changed from her husband?" she asked, her tone light, almost casual. She didn't want to spook Zoe or shut her down.

"I can't say that directly," Zoe replied. "But let's just say the original beneficiary was exactly who you'd expect. The updated one, not so much."

Amelia leaned more heavily against the wall. "So someone... unexpected stood to gain."

"Exactly," Zoe said. "And with the police involved, the claim is on hold while everything gets sorted out. Standard procedure whenever a death is flagged for investigation."

Amelia closed her eyes for a moment, letting the information sink in. This changed things. It changed everything.

"Do you think the new beneficiary knows they were added?" she asked quietly, almost afraid of the answer.

Zoe paused again, and when she spoke, her voice carried a low, knowing humor.

"If they didn't before," she said, "they do now. The police ask a lot of very direct questions."

That made Amelia pause. "So they've already spoken to the new beneficiary?"

"I assume so," Zoe said. "She already had her hands full with her high-profile business. It's tough to keep out of the public eye even without a murder investigation circling."

"She," Amelia repeated softly.

Zoe didn't take the bait. "*Them*. Let's just say... They and Evelyn weren't on friendly terms. Not for a while. But you know Evelyn. She had a way of turning enemies into opportunities. Or into traps."

Amelia's brain tugging at threads that hadn't quite connected until now.

Someone Evelyn had argued with. Someone who'd wanted her gone, or wanted her silence. But then Evelyn had left them something. Not a thank-you. A burden.

"Zoe," Amelia said slowly, "do you think... whoever it was... knew they'd been added?"

Zoe was quiet for a beat. "It's hard to say. But if they didn't know before, I'm sure they do now. And based on what I've heard, they're not exactly happy about it. Whatever Evelyn was planning, it wasn't kindness."

Amelia nodded slowly, more to herself than to Zoe.

"Thanks," she said. "You've been more helpful than you know."

"Just don't name me in your memoir," Zoe said with a wink in her tone. "And seriously, tell Lila I want a cupcake the size of my regrets."

"I'll put in a good word."

After they hung up, Amelia stood for a moment in the hush of the hallway, the hum of the kitchen behind her and the storm of thoughts ahead.

She didn't know who Evelyn had named. But she knew what kind of person it had to be.

Someone high profile. Someone publicly at odds with Evelyn. Someone who'd just been handed a reason to panic.

Now Amelia just had to figure out which of Evelyn's enemies had been turned into her final move.

CHAPTER ELEVEN

AMELIA ARRIVED at Food Truck Alley earlier than usual.

She hadn't planned it that way. But she'd woken before her alarm, eyes wide open and heart already drumming with restless energy. Too many thoughts, too much adrenaline. A quiet breakfast hadn't helped. A steaming mug of tea had only warmed her hands, not her mind. Even the long, hot shower, the kind that usually gave her clarity, had left her no more grounded than before.

There was something about that morning. A tension in the air that she couldn't quite put her finger on. So she'd left the house early, hoping the rhythm of routine might quiet the static. A head start at the truck, some alone time with her checklist and prep work may help her push the noise aside.

Normally, at this hour, Food Truck Alley was only beginning to stir. Vendors would be arriving in ones and twos, the occasional truck engine humming to life, cart wheels clattering as someone wrestled a prep table into place. The air would carry the first notes of bacon grease and frying onions from the breakfast trucks. Someone always had music playing way too early. Usually something upbeat and aggressively cheerful, like bubblegum pop or a song with too much bass. There'd be laughter, muttered swearing, and someone trying to fix a broken shelf with duct tape and sheer optimism.

But today, Amelia pulled into her usual space and immediately frowned. The lot was still. Not quite empty, but too quiet. The usual buzz of morning startup was missing. A few trucks were parked at odd angles, their windows still shuttered.

She scanned the space, but it wasn't the lack of life that set her nerves on edge. It was her own truck.

The Pink Cupcake stood under the soft gray canopy of the morning sky, its cheerful pastel paint slightly dulled in the overcast light. From a distance, it looked almost peaceful, ready for the day.

But then she saw it. The side door wasn't closed.

Amelia's chest tightened. The sight didn't compute at first. The Pink Cupcake's doors were always locked at night. Always. She was meticulous about it and double-checked every single time.

She parked slowly, her engine still idling as her eyes locked onto the uneven silhouette of the open door. A sliver of dark shadow gaped beneath the curved pink awning, like the truck itself had been cracked open.

The door wasn't just ajar. The frame was twisted. The metal around the lock looked warped, as if someone had pried it loose with force. It hadn't been left open by accident. Someone had broken in.

Her stomach dropped, the feeling swift and sickening. Her hand reached instinctively for her phone, already pulling up Dan's contact. But her thumb hesitated above the screen. The rational thing would have been to call him and wait for backup.

But something else flared in her chest instead. Stubbornness. Or maybe something closer to anger.

Whoever had done this hadn't just broken into her truck. They'd invaded her space, her livelihood, her sense of safety. And she wasn't going to let them win by making her retreat.

She shoved the phone into her jacket pocket and opened the glove compartment. Her fingers curled around the heavy-duty flashlight she kept tucked there for late nights and power outages. It was solid in her hand. A small bit of control.

Then she stepped out of the car.

The wind caught her hair as she crossed the lot, her footsteps crunching over gravel. The air was brisk, the early chill biting against her skin, but she barely felt it.

Her fingers brushed the bent edge of the door as she stepped inside. The Pink Cupcake had always been a place of comfort. The smell of vanilla and sugar, the soft pinks and buttery yellows, the hum of mixers and laughter. It was her haven.

Now it was wrecked.

Amelia crouched in the center of the truck, the flashlight still in her hand even though she didn't need it anymore. Daylight streamed through the windows now, catching on the flour that dusted the floor like snowdrifts. It might have looked beautiful, like a sugar-coated winter scene, if not for the churn of chaos that surrounded her.

The ingredient bins were overturned, their contents spilling across the floor in uneven piles. Measuring spoons were scattered like confetti, some bent, others half-buried in flour. The refrigerator door stood wide open, its shelves ransacked, contents spoiled and pooling onto the metal floor in sticky puddles.

Amelia rose slowly, eyes scanning the wreckage. There was no order to the mess. No sign that someone had been looking for something specific. This wasn't theft. It was violation.

Either way, someone had gone to a lot of trouble to make sure she knew: she was a target now.

She stood still, surrounded by the wreckage of her business. She barely registered the approaching footsteps until Lila climbed up into the truck, the clang of her boots against the metal step echoing louder than it should have. Her ponytail was slightly crooked, like she'd dressed in a hurry, but her eyes sharpened the instant she took in the scene.

Lila didn't speak right away. She stood at the threshold for a long beat, letting her gaze travel across the damage: flour smeared like footprints on the floor, the chaos of upturned bins, the refrigerator door yawning open like a wound. She stepped further in, movements quiet and deliberate, eyes flicking from corner to corner.

Then she saw the still-locked cash box, sitting untouched in its corner. The ovens, unscathed. The mixer, unmoved. And Beatrice's vintage piping tips, strewn across the linoleum like some kind of sad parade.

They knew what those tips meant to Beatrice, how carefully they were stored. How Beatrice polished them like they were family heirlooms.

"Did they take anything?" Lila asked.

"I don't think so," Amelia murmured. "I think they were just trying to scare me."

Lila crouched beside the toppled ingredient bins, running her fingers through the thin layer of sugar and cocoa powder that coated the floor. The dust clung to her fingertips, soft and gritty at once. She stared down at her hand like it might offer an answer.

"First your tires," she murmured. "Now this?"

Her mouth set into a thin, tight line.

Another thump echoed from the doorway. Beatrice stepped up into the truck, her arms crossed tightly against her chest. She took one look at the disaster and didn't blink. Her face was unreadable, jaw locked, but her eyes burned.

She moved slowly, surveying the space. Then she pointed, wordlessly, toward the ovens. The mixer. The cash box.

"They could've destroyed the ovens," she said. Her tone was flat, but her words cut like glass.

"Could've taken the mixer. Or the cash box. But they didn't."

Lila nodded grimly. Her boots crunched faintly against the scattered sugar as she moved.

"Because it wasn't from a robber," she said.

Beatrice's lips pressed into a thin line. Her voice dropped even lower. "They want to see if she's going to back down."

She tilted her head toward Amelia, never breaking eye contact.

"This?" she said, gesturing to the chaos around them. "This was a line in the sand. And now they're watching to see she's going to cross it."

The words landed like a weight. Amelia already knew she was being watched, but this confirmed it.

Lila let out a slow breath through her nose. "And are you?" she asked.

Amelia blinked. "What?"

Lila tilted her head, voice soft but pointed. "Going to cross it. Because I know you, Amelia. And I know you're already past the point of turning back."

Beatrice snorted from near the mixer, the sound dry and laced with something fiercer than amusement. "If they think this is going to scare you off, they don't know you at all."

Amelia rubbed her temple, trying to ease the ache building behind her eyes. Her exhaustion was emotional, mental, the wear and tear of being pulled in every direction and asked to stay steady.

Even with three people inside, it suddenly felt cavernous. Amelia let the silence hold for a few more seconds, then glanced up, her tone shifting.

"Zoe called me last night. I didn't get a chance to tell you yet."

Lila straightened, surprised. "What? When?"

"After dinner," Amelia said. "I didn't want to text it. And with the kids around..."

Beatrice raised an eyebrow, arms still crossed. "And?"

Amelia drew in a steady breath.

"She couldn't tell me everything. But she hinted that Evelyn changed the beneficiary on her life insurance policy. Recently."

"Changed it from Graham?" Lila asked, her brow knitting as the implication settled in.

Amelia nodded. "To someone else," she confirmed. "Zoe said the police have already spoken to the new beneficiary. Someone who was already on rocky terms with Evelyn."

Beatrice's eyes narrowed, the gears clearly

turning behind them. "So whoever it is, they've got motive."

"Maybe," Amelia said, letting the word hang in the air. "Or maybe Evelyn wanted to make it look that way. She was capable of that. Either way, someone benefits."

Lila crossed her arms. "So this break-in is not some random act of vandalism. It's someone trying to shake you off the trail."

Amelia let her gaze drift across the truck again, the overturned bins, the scattered tools, the deliberate mess of it all. There was a rhythm to the destruction, but also an eerie restraint. So much had been wrecked, and yet so much had been purposefully left untouched.

Beatrice let out a slow breath through her nose, stepping forward to get a better view of the wreckage. Her eyes moved with a baker's precision, taking in every displaced spoon, every ruined container.

"I hate that they touched my piping tips," she muttered, the words almost lost beneath her breath. "Vandalism is one thing. But that I take personally."

Amelia managed a small smile. "Everything about this was personal," she murmured. "Whoever did this, they wanted me to feel it."

She leaned back against the counter, only then

noticing the deep ache in her shoulders. Her arms hung heavy at her sides. The adrenaline that had carried her this far was draining fast, leaving behind only a mind full of static.

"Maybe the police are already closing in," Amelia said quietly. "They have the beneficiary info now. They've talked to this person. They've seen what Evelyn did. Maybe they'll get to the bottom of it soon."

Lila tilted her head slightly, eyes on Amelia. "Do you believe that?"

Amelia hesitated. "I want to."

Beatrice arched an eyebrow. "But?"

Amelia exhaled slowly. "But I'm the one who saw the way Evelyn operated. Up close. I'm the one who's talked to the people she manipulated. The ones she hurt."

She paused, her gaze dropping for a moment before rising again.

"I don't want to be the one carrying this," she said. "I didn't ask for any of it, but it feels like I already am."

She stepped across the truck and reached for the open door. Her fingers wrapped around the edge of it, and she pulled it shut with care.

"I'll call Dan," she said over her shoulder. "I have to report the break-in."

Lila's voice followed her, curious but light. "You think he'll be mad you didn't call him first?"

Amelia turned, offering a weary smile that didn't quite reach her eyes. "Oh, he'll definitely be mad," she said. "But he'll get over it. He always does."

Beatrice shifted her weight, leaning her hip against the prep table. "So, should we sweep up? Or leave it for crime scene photos?"

Amelia sighed. "Let's leave it."

She stepped down from the truck and pulled her phone from her pocket, thumb hovering over Dan's name.

For now, she'd play it straight. Let the police do their job, give them a chance to catch up. But deep down, a familiar voice whispered:

You're already ahead. Keep going.

Amelia exhaled and hit "Call."

CHAPTER TWELVE

DETECTIVE WALTER HOBBS showed up a little while after Dan arrived. Inside, the truck looked no better than it had when she found it. Flour still coated the floors, like a dusting of snow after a blizzard.

Amelia leaned against the truck's outer panel, doing her best not to pace.

"No theft," Hobbs said after he came out. "Not even a busted appliance."

"Nope," Amelia replied. "Just chaos."

"Looks like intimidation," Dan said. "Same as the tires."

Amelia nodded, though the knot in her stomach twisted tighter at the thought. She'd been telling herself she could handle this, that she was tougher than whoever was trying to scare her, but that didn't make the fear any less real.

Hobbs turned to face her fully now, his arms crossed over his chest. His expression was calm, but there was a sharpness in his eyes that said he wasn't going to let this pass without answers. "Mind telling me what you think is going on here?"

Amelia didn't flinch under his gaze. She took a breath, the cool air filling her lungs.

"Someone's warning me off," she said. "I've been asking questions about Evelyn Waters. I'm getting close, apparently."

Hobbs arched an eyebrow at that. "And what do you think you're close to?"

Amelia hesitated, just for a moment, but she pushed her words forward anyway. "I think someone had a reason to want Evelyn gone," she said. "I think that person might've benefited from it financially."

Hobbs watched her carefully. "You think this is about money?"

Amelia nodded. "Evelyn had enemies, sure. But she also had leverage. She filed lawsuits, stirred up trouble, made threats. She didn't let things go. Then, out of nowhere, she drops a lawsuit against someone with a lot of money and a very public business, doesn't ask for a payout, doesn't go to trial. She just... walks away."

For a moment, the only sounds were the distant murmur of the morning traffic and the soft creak of the truck's metal panels as they cooled in the chill. Then Hobbs spoke again. "Kimberly Reeves," he said.

Amelia blinked at the sound of it, surprised to hear him say it aloud.

"I figured it was her," Amelia said carefully, masking the spark of satisfaction in her tone. "It didn't make sense otherwise. Evelyn never gave up on anything unless she got something better in return."

Dan's hands were in his pockets, but he stayed quiet. His eyes moved between Amelia and Hobbs.

Amelia felt a determination hardening in her chest. "I've seen Evelyn work," she said. "She doesn't drop anything unless she gets something bigger in return. So I started wondering, what if she didn't get money? What if she got power?"

"Power how?" Hobbs asked.

"By changing her life insurance policy," she said. "Graham was the beneficiary. But he's not anymore, is he?"

Hobbs didn't blink. His expression didn't

change, but she could tell by the slight pause that he wasn't surprised by her words. "No," he said simply. "She changed it. A few weeks before her death."

The pieces were starting to fall into place, but the picture was still blurred at the edges.

"She changed it," Hobbs repeated. "But that doesn't make the new beneficiary the killer."

"Doesn't mean they're not," Amelia said. She wasn't about to let Hobbs dismiss the angle without at least considering it.

Hobbs let out a short sigh. "We looked into it," he said. "Thoroughly. Alibi checks out. No signs of contact before or after Evelyn's death. If anything, the change caught her off guard."

"So you think Evelyn set her up?" Amelia asked, her brow furrowing. It made a twisted kind of sense.

"I think Evelyn liked chaos," he said. "She liked making people squirm. You think it's a reward. Maybe it was punishment."

Dan frowned. "But that doesn't explain the break-in," he said.

"No," Hobbs agreed, his tone turning thoughtful as he nodded slowly, his eyes flicking back toward the busted door. "That part's newer and more personal."

He looked back at Amelia then. "You're poking

at something," he said. "Just be smart about how far you take it."

She stayed quiet for a moment. The sounds of the street outside seemed muffled as she contemplated.

"You said the change caught the new beneficiary off guard," Amelia said. She could feel her thoughts speeding up now, the momentum building. "And to remove your husband from your policy right before you die is calculated. Kimberly was rattled when I talked to her. She has a business to protect, her reputation, events to manage. If Evelyn had something on her, or was threatening to go public... maybe Kimberly pushed back. Maybe Evelyn flipped the game and put her name on the policy to tie her in, and make sure if something happened, people would look at her." She paused, letting her words settle in the heavy air. "If I were Evelyn, maybe that's what I would do."

Hobbs gave her a look, part weary, part appreciative of her tenacity. "That's the theory we're working with," he said. "We don't have anything solid yet. Nothing that ties it all together, nothing that would stick in court."

"And Kimberly really said she didn't know?" Amelia asked.

"She was surprised," Hobbs said, his brow furrowing slightly as he recalled the details. "Legally, it's allowed. You don't have to tell someone you've named them in a policy. It's your right to change the beneficiary."

"So you believe her?" Amelia pressed.

"I believe she didn't kill Evelyn," Hobbs said slowly. "At least not directly." He paused, his gaze flicking over her shoulder, back to the truck behind them. The broken door, the flour scattered like white ash. "But this—" he gestured with a small tilt of his chin "—this makes me think there's more to the story."

Amelia nodded. "But why her?" she murmured again, more to herself than to him. "Why would Evelyn choose Kimberly?"

Hobbs sighed, the sound long and low, as if he'd been turning that question over in his mind for days. "We've been asking the same thing. It doesn't make sense on paper."

"She sued her," Amelia murmured. "Evelyn liked control. Maybe she thought tying Kimberly to the money would force her into something down the road. Evelyn liked being the one pulling the strings."

"Yes," Hobbs agreed. "She'd trap someone just to see how long they'd squirm. But, again, we talked to

Kimberly already, interviewed her twice. She was genuinely shocked. And—" he paused for emphasis, letting the word hang between them "—she was at a client tasting the day Evelyn died. Five people confirmed it. Solid."

"So you're ruling her out completely?" Amelia asked.

"As the killer? Yes," Hobbs said, his tone final. "As someone who might've been pulled into something she didn't fully understand? That's a different story."

Amelia stayed quiet, letting it all settle in her chest. Kimberly might not be the killer, but that didn't mean she wasn't at the center of this. And it didn't mean she was safe from whoever was still out there, still trying to keep the last secrets hidden. The real killer was still out there.

CHAPTER THIRTEEN

THE HOUSE WAS QUIET. The kids were already at school, their empty bowls drying in the sink. Dan had kissed her goodbye a little after eight and left with his favorite travel mug in hand. He had smiled at her over his shoulder before slipping out the door, the click of the latch echoing in the hallway.

Now it was just Amelia. A mug of coffee warmed her palms as she stood barefoot in the kitchen, letting the steam rise up and curl around her face. It should have been peaceful. But instead, her kitchen table was a battlefield.

Notebooks, pens, and legal pads were spread out across the surface with her handwriting scrawled on the pages. Names were circled and underlined, crossed out and rewritten. Diagrams of motives and grudges, arrows zigzagging between them, as though she could map the truth if she just connected the right dots.

She sat hunched over the chaos, her pencil tapping absently against her lips as she stared at the clutter in front of her. She'd written the names in bold, block letters. The list had shrunk, pruned down. Everyone else had been ruled out, dismissed, or frightened off. Some were too far removed from Evelyn's final days to be worth pressing. But two names remained at the center of her scribbled web.

Kimberly. Graham.

Both had reason to hate Evelyn. Both had been tangled in her chaos until the very end. Amelia flipped back a page in her notes, smoothing the paper with her palm.

Kimberly had been publicly humiliated, accused, sued. Then, oddly, absolved. Evelyn had dropped the lawsuit without explanation. Weeks later, Evelyn was dead, and Kimberly was the sole beneficiary of her life insurance policy, a payout Kimberly claimed she hadn't known about.

Amelia circled Kimberly's name again, adding a fresh question mark beside it. Could Kimberly have worked with someone to kill Evelyn?

Amelia's tires had been slashed after visiting

Kimberly last time. Not to mention the recent vandalism in her food truck. That level of intimidation didn't feel like Kimberly's style. She would have needed help. Someone to get their hands dirty while she stayed polished and composed.

Could she have been working with Graham?

She shifted in her seat, stretching her legs, feeling the cold wood floor under her toes as she flipped to the other page. Graham's name loomed in her notes. The ex-husband. The ghost of a man sitting in that diner. No tears. Just a hollow bitterness and a half-empty coffee cup. Amelia scribbled beneath his name:

Broke

Cut out of the policy

Publicly ignored by Evelyn

No visible grief

Alibi

He looked like someone used up and discarded. But what if he hadn't been left behind at all? What if Evelyn had underestimated him?

She snapped the notebook shut, the sound loud in the stillness. It was time to pay Kimberly Reeves another visit. This time, she was going to push.

Reeves & Co. Catering was already buzzing when Amelia arrived mid-morning. The entire space moved like a well-oiled machine, an orchestra of precision and order. Crisp white uniforms blurred between open prep stations, their movements brisk and efficient. Amelia smelled the layered scent of browned butter, rosemary, and something slightly citrusy baking in the back ovens, blending into a perfume of polished professionalism.

Sleek countertops gleamed under the overhead lights. Every utensil was in its place. The floors were spotless, not a single breadcrumb or stray smudge in sight. It was why Amelia had picked now, the mid-shift, mid-week, when the kitchen would be bustling with staff, clipboard-wielding coordinators over-seeing trays of delicate canapés, and sous chefs discussing logistics in hushed, focused tones. A very public, very professional setting. She would be safe.

She spotted Kimberly at the far end of the test kitchen, her sharp figure angled toward a young chef as they examined a platter of miniature hors d'oeu-vres. Amelia stayed back, waiting. Finally, Kimberly looked up. Their eyes locked.

Amelia saw a flicker of polite surprise. Then a subtle narrowing of her eyes. The shift in posture, like someone bracing for an unwelcome conversation. But Kimberly didn't falter. She handed the platter back to the chef, murmured something that sent the younger woman bustling away, and then crossed the gleaming kitchen toward Amelia, her heels clicking quietly on the pristine floor.

"If you're here for a tasting," she said, her tone edged with dry professionalism, "you're about three hours early."

Amelia offered a faint, practiced smile of her own. "I'm here to ask a question. Just one."

Kimberly glanced over her shoulder, a quick, discreet scan of the bustling kitchen, then gestured for Amelia to follow her toward a narrow side hallway. The space was lined with neatly labeled spice racks, hanging copper pans polished to a mirror shine, and an undercurrent of fresh lemon cleanser that clung to the walls.

"I already told the police everything I know," Kimberly said.

Amelia nodded. "I believe you. I think you told them exactly what you thought they needed to hear."

Kimberly's jaw tightened, the only crack in her composure so far.

Amelia didn't press her advantage yet. She kept her tone light. "I don't think you told them everything."

Kimberly's stance said confidence, but the tension in her shoulders whispered something else. "Careful, Mrs. Walishovsky. You're inching toward slander."

Amelia let the corner of her mouth lift into a small, knowing smile. "I'm inching toward the truth. And I think you're tired of holding it in."

A long pause stretched between them. The quiet hum of the kitchen faded as the sounds of the busy world receded behind them.

Then Kimberly let out a short breath, almost a laugh, but brittle, tight at the edges. "This is ridiculous."

"Is it?" Amelia pressed, her voice dropping to a gentler register. She took a slow, deliberate step forward, bridging the distance between them. "Evelyn sued you. She tried to drag your name through the mud. And then, without a settlement, she dropped it. That's not who she was. Evelyn never let go unless she got something bigger."

Kimberly looked away, her gaze fixing on a row of neatly stacked silver pans. Her silence spoke volumes.

Amelia took another step closer. "And now we know she made you the beneficiary on her policy."

Kimberly flinched.

"You didn't kill her," Amelia said softly. "But you know more than you told the police. And if you're worried about what that means, don't be. I'm not here to arrest you. I want to understand why Evelyn did it."

"She said it was a joke," Kimberly murmured. "A stupid, theatrical idea. She said she was going to disappear. Fake her death and make it look like an accident."

Amelia's breath caught in her throat. The audacity of it and sheer recklessness was so perfectly Evelyn.

Kimberly shook her head, eyes distant, like she could still hear Evelyn pitching the idea in that self-important tone. "She said I'd be the one to collect the insurance money," Kimberly went on, her voice barely above a whisper now. "And when it cleared, I'd wire a portion to a Cayman account she gave me. She swore it would all be anonymous. That she'd vanish, live off the grid."

Amelia stared at her. "And you believed her?"

Kimberly let out a bitter laugh. "Of course not. I thought it was another one of her manipulations. Maybe even to make me look guilty if things went south."

She pressed her fingers hard into her skin, as if

she could massage away the memory. Her voice cracked slightly. "She had a way of making you think you were crazy for doubting her."

"So you agreed?"

Kimberly's lips twisted into a grim smile. "I didn't agree. I... didn't stop her. I only humored her because she promised to drop the lawsuit. She was exhausting. I thought, fine, let her fantasize. She'd drop it eventually."

"Was she about to go ahead with it?"

"I don't know. I wasn't in touch with her after that. I thought it was all so ludicrous and I didn't want anything to do with her or her schemes."

Amelia took a slow step back. "But someone stopped her before she could act on it."

Kimberly nodded wearily. "And now I look like the one who had everything to gain."

Kimberly sagged slightly against the stainless steel prep table behind her, as if it was siphoning the last of her strength. She didn't look nearly as composed as before.

"I told myself it was a joke," she repeated, more to herself now than to Amelia. Her voice faltered, hoarse and thin. "A stupid, theatrical idea. Like something out of a made-for-TV movie. She always did have a flair for the dramatic. She swore it would be easy and that she'd vanish, live off the grid."

Amelia took another step back, giving Kimberly some space. Even though Evelyn had been a thorn in her side, Kimberly clearly felt bad about her death.

"What about Graham?" Amelia asked gently.

Kimberly blinked, confusion flickering across her face. "What about him?"

"Do you think he knew about Evelyn's plan?"

Kimberly shook her head after considering the question. "Not that I'm aware of," she said slowly. "Evelyn barely mentioned him to me. Honestly, I think she considered him irrelevant."

Amelia absorbed that. "Could he have found out about the policy change?"

Kimberly frowned, considering it longer this time. "I suppose anything's possible."

Amelia nodded slowly, the wheels in her head grinding forward. "If he did find out she'd cut him out..."

Kimberly gave a faint, uncertain shrug. "Sure. That would be a blow. But I don't see what he stood to gain from killing her. The money would go to me, not him."

"So you don't think it was him?"

"I don't know what to think," she admitted, her

voice thin and stripped of bravado. "But Graham never struck me as the type. He was just... pathetic. Not violent."

"Someone made sure Evelyn wouldn't follow through with her plan," Amelia said quietly, almost to herself. "Someone who didn't want her to vanish."

Kimberly looked away sharply, her posture curling in, like she wanted to disappear herself. "Whoever that was, they're still out there."

Amelia gave Kimberly a final nod. "Thanks for telling me the truth."

Kimberly's lips pressed into a thin line. "I hope it helps," she said softly.

CHAPTER FOURTEEN

THE PINK CUPCAKE sat under a parking lot floodlight, its normally cheerful pink exterior washed out to a sad, chalky gray in the evening haze. The usual whimsical lettering on the side panels looked ghostly now, distorted by the shadows that stretched and curled along the alley walls.

Food Truck Alley, usually bursting with sizzling grills, clattering spatulas, and the low hum of laughter and gossip, was silent tonight. Even the new taco truck, the one that always overstayed its welcome, pumping salsa music into the night air and keeping the party going long past last call, was gone. The place felt abandoned, like a carnival after closing.

Amelia lingered outside the truck longer than

she needed to, her eyes tracing the curves of the cupcake logo like she was memorizing it for the last time. The only sounds she heard were the faint rustle of dry leaves and the persistent buzz of the overhead light.

She inhaled deeply and squared her shoulders, forcing herself to move forward. She climbed the small steps and entered the truck. Her fingers tightened around the manila folder she carried.

Inside, the air was cool and smelled faintly of vanilla. She reached for the dim overhead lights, flicking them on. They buzzed and stuttered before settling into a weak, flickering glow that only seemed to highlight the empty spaces. The metal floor felt colder under her shoes tonight. Each step echoed back at her. She could feel her own heartbeat in the silence, a steady thump that sounded too loud in her ears.

At the small counter near the register, she sat down, letting the folder rest against the cold stainless steel. With slow, deliberate movements, she unpacked its contents, each page covered in Evelyn's jagged handwriting. The words were as chaotic and messy as the woman herself had been, with anger bleeding through every loop and flourish. The fake ID clipped to the top looked so real in the half-light, the lamination catching the pale glow like a mocking wink.

It was all staged, a carefully arranged performance for the final act.

But even knowing that, Amelia's breath felt tight in her chest. Because she knew someone was out there, watching and waiting. And tonight, there would be no turning back.

She rubbed her arms, trying to shake off the chill that had settled there the second she stepped into the truck. Outside, the wind picked up, sending a stray napkin skittering across the pavement like a startled mouse darting for cover.

She tried not to glance at the clock again, though the impulse gnawed at her. Instead, she forced herself to stay focused on the performance. She picked up one of the sheets, holding it up to the flickering light. She squinted like she was searching for buried secrets, pretending to puzzle out patterns no one else had seen.

Really, she wasn't searching for anything. She already knew what the papers said. They were nothing more than bait. But if anyone was watching, it had to look real. Her hand trembled slightly. She steadied it, drawing in a breath that felt too shallow.

From the periphery, she noticed movement: a

shadow low to the ground, shifting forward, then back.

Her breath hitched, caught still in her chest. She didn't dare turn and look. She kept flipping through the papers, her eyes fixed on the meaningless scribbles. She forced her breathing to stay steady, though her heartbeat was a thunderclap in her ears, loud enough she was sure he could hear it too.

Then another sound, a footstep, closer now.

The hair on the back of her neck prickled upright. She could feel the heat of someone standing behind her, the faintest shift of the air in the cramped space. The sharp smell of cologne so out of place in the sugar-scented truck.

Then she heard his voice.

"Amelia."

She turned, deliberately slow, forcing every movement to stay calm.

Graham Waters stood just inside the truck, framed by the doorway. The metal lip creaked faintly beneath his weight as the side door hung ajar, the chill wind tugging at the edge of his coat. His face was pale, almost waxy, the shadows under his eyes so deep they looked bruised. But it was his eyes that froze her. They were darker than she remembered, brimming with a mixture of desperation and rage that burned so much she could almost feel it against her skin.

"You shouldn't be here," he said.

Amelia swallowed, keeping her voice even. She felt the weight of every word before it left her mouth.

"Neither should you."

Graham's gaze dropped to the papers spread across the counter. His brow furrowed as his attention locked onto the fake ID clipped to the top, his jaw tightening.

"You found something?" he asked.

"Depends," she said. "What are you afraid I found?"

Graham's nostrils flared. He took a step forward. Then another, his boots scraping softly on the metal floor. His eyes burned into hers, the crackling tension between them thrumming like an electric current.

"You don't know what she was like," he said, his voice rising. "What she did to me."

The words spilled out of him in ragged breaths. His face twisted with something raw and ugly.

"You think Evelyn was just some loudmouth scam artist? She was worse. She twisted everything. She ruined me. She left me with nothing."

Amelia's voice was soft but steady. "She didn't deserve to die."

"She wasn't going to die," he spat, "Unless I did something about it."

The confession snapped out of him before he could stop it. Graham blinked, his face freezing for a fraction of a second. In that blink, she saw the flicker of realization. He'd said too much, and he knew it, but there was no way to take it back now.

Amelia let the silence stretch, let him keep talking.

"She was going to disappear," he said. "That was her grand plan. Vanish and start over. New life, new name, new everything. On someone else's dime. On *mine*. She cut me out like I didn't exist."

He took another step forward, his voice cracking under the weight of everything he'd kept inside. His face was flushed, sweat glistening along his hairline.

"After everything I put up with. After everything I gave her. She was going to leave me behind with the debts and the shame. She was going to make me look like a fool. And she was going to laugh while she did it."

The words were tumbling out of him in a rush now, as if the dam had finally cracked. His shoulders hunched, and he looked down at the fake documents spread across the counter. His fingers twitched at his sides, curling into fists before relaxing again, caught in a cycle he couldn't stop.

"No," he said, his voice barely above a whisper now, choked with something close to grief. "I couldn't let her do that. I couldn't."

His hand hovered over the counter, his fingers flexing like he wanted to crush the papers.

"You weren't supposed to find this," he muttered, his voice spiraling into a bitter hiss. "You weren't supposed to dig this deep."

His hand twitched again, inching closer to the folder as if he could still somehow snatch it back and erase everything he'd just said.

But Amelia's hand moved too, not toward the papers, but the panic button under the register. She didn't have to press it for the unmistakable clatter of heavy boots to stomp into the truck.

"Graham Waters," came Detective Hobbs' voice. "Don't move."

Two officers appeared behind Hobbs at the side door, their weapons drawn but held low. They didn't have to point them. The weight of their presence was enough.

Graham froze, his hands hovering higher above the fake file. His fingers curled like claws, trembling in the air.

"Step back," Hobbs ordered, his tone calm, cold, final.

For a moment, Amelia thought Graham might still do something desperate. His fingers were flexing in the air like he was weighing one last, reckless move. Her heart hammered against her ribs, and she could almost see it happening, the desperate lunge, the final attempt to snatch back control.

But then he crumbled. His shoulders dropped all at once. The last thread holding him together snapped, and the fight drained from him so completely it was almost eerie. The man who'd entered the truck with such simmering fury was gone. In his place stood someone utterly defeated, hollowed out by the weight of what he'd done and what he'd lost.

"You don't understand," he muttered. It was more to himself than anyone else. "She was going to erase me, like I was never part of her life."

The words echoed in the cold air. Hobbs didn't flinch. He moved forward, and so did his officers.

"You erased her first," Hobbs said, reaching for Graham's wrists.

Graham didn't protest. He just stared at the floor. Hobbs secured the cuffs with practiced ease and stepped back.

Behind him, Dan stepped into the truck. His eyes swept over Graham once, then shifted to Amelia, finding her in the dim light. He scanned her face, her posture, the slight tremor in her hands, checking for damage, for fear.

She gave him a faint, tired smile. It was all she had left. A small, weary sign that she was still standing.

"I told you I'd be careful," she said softly.

Dan didn't smile back, but he did take her hand, his grip firm and grounding. It was enough to pull her back from the edge she hadn't realized she'd been teetering on.

"And I told you I'd be watching," he said quietly, his words carrying more weight than she could admit.

Outside, the wind picked up again, rattling the thin metal of the truck and sending a swirl of dead leaves skittering across the lot. The danger was over, but the echoes of it still clung to the walls.

With Graham led away in cuffs, and the worst of it behind them, Amelia knew the cleanup was just beginning.

CHAPTER FIFTEEN

THE PINK CUPCAKE smelled like vanilla, sugar, and the faintest trace of orange zest left over from the early morning's batch of cupcakes. The scent wrapped around Amelia like a comfort blanket, settling into her chest and easing the last of the tightness that had lived there for far too long. Today, she felt something close to peace. Gone was the tension of being stalked by a murderer, as well as the low hum of dread that had buzzed in the back of her mind every time she locked up for the night.

Beatrice was already wrist-deep in batter, sleeves pushed up, moving with her usual methodical rhythm. She hummed a tune under her breath, the quiet sound almost blending with the gentle whoosh of the oven fan.

At the front of the truck, Lila flipped the open sign with a practiced flick of her wrist. Amelia sat at the back counter, tucked into her usual spot. She cradled her coffee with both hands, the heat seeping into her palms.

For a few moments, she let herself feel the stillness, and the warm air and the comforting smells soak into her bones. The danger was past them now, the worst of it left behind in the dark corners of memory. And in the quiet of the early morning, she could almost believe it was just another day. Just cupcakes and coffee.

Then the truck's side door creaked open, the faint groan of metal shifting breaking the soft spell. Dan stepped in first, his gaze sweeping the room the way it always did, measuring everything, cataloging exits, blind spots, anything out of place. Old habits didn't fade easily, not after the week they'd had. Behind him came Detective Hobbs, his expression still no-nonsense, though there was a faint glimmer of relief at the corners of his eyes.

"We're just here to grab the gear," Dan said, tipping his chin toward the back wall where all the surveillance equipment had been installed just days ago.

Amelia raised a brow, already half-smiling despite herself. "Already?"

Hobbs made his way straight to the paper towel dispenser and began carefully detaching the tiny microphone embedded beside it. Dan crouched near the lower cabinets, looking for the neatly coiled wires that snaked behind the counter. He shot Amelia a knowing glance over his shoulder, a small grin tugging at his lips as he reached for the first wire.

"You weren't thinking of keeping it, were you?" he asked.

Amelia took a long, unbothered sip of her coffee. "What, like a souvenir?"

"Or for future use," Lila chimed in. "Don't act like you weren't already thinking of making it a permanent feature."

Beatrice didn't look up from her bowl, her spoon moving in slow, even circles through the batter. "We could call it the Sprinkle Cam. Catch people sneaking free frosting when they think no one's watching."

Hobbs was now unscrewing the pinhole camera hidden just above the shelf near the register.

"You can have your frosting surveillance after we finish booking the guy who tried to kill you," he said.

"Small details," Amelia said with a wink. "But

when someone steals my buttercream, I'm calling in a full crime scene team. No half measures when frosting's involved."

Dan chuckled under his breath as he zipped the last cable into the evidence pouch, his shoulders finally relaxing now that the last of the gear was packed away. "You're incorrigible," he said, shaking his head with affectionate disbelief.

"You married it," she replied playfully, a small smile tugging at her lips.

He leaned over, brushing a kiss to her cheek. "Best mistake I ever made," he murmured.

The door creaked again as the two men stepped out into the brightening morning. The metal clicked softly as it shut behind them.

Beatrice paused in her mixing and shot an expectant look across the counter to Amelia. "Alright," she said, her voice calm but firm. "Spill it."

Lila raised an eyebrow, her smirk edged with disbelief. "You're way too calm for someone who almost got murdered in her own food truck," she said.

Amelia set her coffee down with exaggerated care. She turned toward them, a satisfied smile pulling at the corners of her mouth. "I wasn't almost murdered," she said. "Not really."

Beatrice's brow arched high. "What happened?"

Amelia took a breath. "Hobbs and I planned the trap three days ago. I suspected Graham was the one following me, but we needed proof. Something that would hold up."

Lila laughed. "So you lured him into the pink truck? How did you know it was him?"

Amelia shook her head, savoring the chance to finally tell them the whole story. "Once I started connecting the dots—Evelyn's fake death plan, the life insurance beneficiary change, Kimberly's innocence—it all pointed in the same direction. Graham had the most to lose. Or at least, the most anger to burn."

Beatrice's brow furrowed deeper. "How did you lure him in here?" she asked.

"We leaked a rumor at his usual diner," Amelia explained. "Whispers that I'd uncovered some new evidence from Evelyn. We made sure it looked real enough to scare him into acting out."

Lila's eyes widened. "And you knew he was watching you?"

"Hobbs had a few sightings reported in the area, someone matching Graham's description near the truck a few nights earlier," Amelia said. "It wasn't much, but it was enough to make us act. We needed him to think I had the smoking gun."

Beatrice crossed her arms. "And then you just waited here? That must've been terrifying," she said, though her voice was soft with something closer to respect.

"Not alone," Amelia clarified, her voice firm. "We planted microphones and cameras, as you saw. Hobbs and the police were parked close by in an unmarked car, listening in real time. Dan, too. The second Graham made a move, boom. They came and got him."

Lila let out a long, shaky breath and leaned back against the counter, pressing her palms flat against the cool stainless steel like she needed the solidity. "You really did it," she said. "You let him walk right into the net."

Beatrice gave a low whistle.

Amelia gave a modest shrug, though the gleam in her eyes said she wasn't nearly as modest as she pretended. "He was never going to confess at a precinct," she said. "He needed to feel in control, and to think he was smarter than me."

"And instead," Beatrice said, her smile growing into something almost mischievous, "he ended up confessing with a mic under the register and a camera pointed right at him."

"I just set the table," Amelia said with quiet finality. "He brought the mess."

Beatrice cracked a rare, genuine laugh, the sound bright in the cozy space.

"I'm just looking forward to regular problems," Amelia said. "Running out of flour, overcooked cupcakes, that sort of thing."

Lila snorted and shook her head. "But this is Gary," she said, her smile wry. "It's either murder or a cupcake crisis."

"It's true," Beatrice said, still grinning as she resumed her steady stirring. "We can handle either."

Amelia laughed with them. The last of the tension in her body had finally eased out of her shoulders like sugar dissolving in warm tea.

She glanced toward the service window and caught sight of a new customer approaching, wallet already in hand. She straightened her shoulders, wiped her hands on a towel, and stepped forward with a smile that felt lighter than it had in days.

Business as usual.

RECIPE 1: HONEY LAVENDER CUPCAKES

MAKES *12 cupcakes*

Ingredients:

- 1/2 cup (1 stick) unsalted butter, softened
- 1/2 cup granulated sugar
- 1/4 cup honey (preferably floral, like clover or wildflower)
- 2 large eggs, room temperature
- 1 tsp vanilla extract
- 1 1/4 cups all-purpose flour
- 1/2 tsp baking powder
- 1/4 tsp baking soda
- 1/4 tsp salt
- 1/2 cup whole milk

• 1 tbsp dried culinary lavender (lightly crushed with fingers or in a mortar & pestle)

For the Honey Lavender Buttercream:

• 1/2 cup (1 stick) unsalted butter, softened
• 2 cups powdered sugar
• 2 tbsp honey
• 1–2 tbsp milk or cream
• Optional: 1/2 tsp vanilla or a drop of food-grade lavender oil
• Garnish: small lavender buds or edible flowers (optional)

Instructions

Preheat the oven to 350°F (175°C). Line a 12-cup muffin tin with paper liners.

Steep the lavender: Warm the milk gently (don't boil), add the crushed lavender, and let steep for 5–10 minutes. Strain and let cool slightly.

Make the batter. In a large bowl, cream together butter, sugar, and honey until light and fluffy (2–3 minutes). Add eggs one at a time, mixing well after each. Stir in vanilla.

In a separate bowl, whisk together flour, baking

powder, baking soda, and salt. Alternate adding the dry ingredients and lavender-infused milk to the butter mixture, beginning and ending with the dry. Mix until just combined—don't overmix.

Divide the batter evenly among the cupcake liners. Bake for 18–20 minutes, or until a toothpick inserted in the center comes out clean. Let cool completely before frosting.

For the Buttercream:

Beat the butter until smooth and creamy (2 minutes). Add powdered sugar a little at a time. Add honey, milk, and vanilla or lavender oil (if using). Beat until light and fluffy. Adjust consistency with a splash more milk, if needed.

Pipe or spread onto cooled cupcakes. Garnish with a few dried lavender buds or a tiny edible flower if you're feeling fancy.

RECIPE 2: DARK CHOCOLATE RASPBERRY TRUFFLE CUPCAKE

MAKES *12–14 cupcakes*

Ingredients

- 3/4 cup all-purpose flour
- 1/2 cup unsweetened dark cocoa powder
- 3/4 tsp baking soda
- 1/4 tsp salt
- 2 oz bittersweet or dark chocolate, chopped
- 1/2 cup hot coffee (or hot water)
- 1/2 cup buttermilk (room temp)
- 1/2 cup packed brown sugar
- 1/4 cup granulated sugar
- 1/3 cup vegetable oil
- 1 tsp vanilla extract

• 1 large egg (room temp)

For the Raspberry Filling:
• 1 cup fresh or frozen raspberries
• 2 tbsp sugar
• 1 tsp lemon juice
• 1 tbsp cornstarch mixed with 1 tbsp cold water

For the Dark Chocolate Ganache Frosting:
• 6 oz dark chocolate (60–70%), finely chopped
• 1/2 cup heavy cream
• 2 tbsp unsalted butter
• Optional: 1 tbsp raspberry liqueur or Chambord for extra flavor

Optional Garnish:
• Fresh raspberry on top
• Chocolate curls or dust
• Gold sugar pearls (because drama deserves sparkle)

Instructions

Preheat oven to 350°F (175°C). Line a cupcake pan with liners.

In a heatproof bowl, combine chopped chocolate and cocoa powder. Pour hot coffee (or water) over it. Let sit 1 minute, then whisk until smooth. Cool slightly.

In a large bowl, whisk flour, baking soda, and salt. In another bowl, whisk the chocolate mixture with buttermilk, sugars, oil, vanilla, and egg until smooth. Add dry ingredients and mix until just combined.

Fill the liners 2/3 full. Bake for 18–20 minutes or until a toothpick comes out with a few moist crumbs. Cool completely.

Make the Raspberry Filling:

In a small saucepan, combine raspberries, sugar, and lemon juice over medium heat. Stir until raspberries break down. Add cornstarch slurry and stir until thickened (1–2 minutes). Remove from heat and cool.

Once cupcakes are cool, use a small knife or cupcake corer to remove a little plug from the center. Fill with raspberry filling (a small spoon or piping bag works well). Replace the tops.

. . .

Make the Ganache Frosting:

In a small saucepan, heat cream and butter just until it starts to simmer. Pour over chopped chocolate in a bowl. Let sit 1 minute, then whisk until smooth. Stir in raspberry liqueur if using.

Let it cool until thickened to a spreadable consistency (or chill and whip for a fluffier texture).

Frost the cupcakes generously. Top with a raspberry, chocolate curl, or whatever flair your murder-solving heart desires.

These are best slightly chilled.

ABOUT THE AUTHOR

Harper Lin is a *USA TODAY* bestselling cozy mystery author. When she's not reading or writing mysteries, she loves going to yoga classes, hiking, and baking with her family and friends.

For a complete list of her books by series, visit her website.

www.HarperLin.com